Once Upon a Time

Alane Hotchkin

Once Upon a Time

Alane Hotchkin

Affinity
eBook Press
NZ
2015

Once upon a Time

© Alane Hotchkin 2015

Affinity E-Book Press NZ LTD
Canterbury, New Zealand

1st Edition

ISBN: 978-0-908351-28-2

All rights reserved.

Editor: Ruth Stanley
Proof Editor: Alexis Smith
Cover Design: Irish Dragon Designs

Acknowledgments

First and foremost I have to thank all of those that have stood by me and bought my first published books. I promise you there are many more to come.

A huge thank you to Julie, Mel, and Nancy for taking me into their publishing circle. Nancy, most awesome cover—thank you. Thank you also for your editing and helping me to see the light instead of fading to black.

As always a big thank-you to my beta readers, you are fantastic. The task of keeping me sane on a day-to-day basis award goes to two people. Without TJ and my wife Sarah life would be dull as a brick. You two rock!

Dedication

Who doesn't love a pirate story? I wrote this book for all of us women who have dreamed of being found by a gorgeous, hellfire of a pirate.

One magical day I found my pirate and married her.

This one's for you, babe.

I love you…

Table of Contents

Also by Alane Hotchkin

The Ball, The Blackhawk Chronicles Introduction

Beginning of the End, Book One Blackhawk Chronicles

My Everything, Book Two Blackhawk Chronicles

Prologue

"Mama, tell us a story."

Lying beneath the quilts were two mischievous raven-haired twin girls. All that gazed upon them did so in wonder. How could they look so innocent, yet be such little terrors? The villagers thought the twins to be the most beautiful children ever born to the royal bloodline.

The queen carefully sat on the edge of the bed. "What kind of story shall we have tonight, my angels?" She pulled the covers up around their necks to ward off the chill in the room, as the fire died down in the fireplace. She could not believe they were six seasons old already. It seemed they were born only a sunrise ago.

Their foreheads touching, the girls whispered to each other. Since their first words were uttered, Rhiannon spoke for both of them. "Tell us the story about the princess and the pirate that saved her again. Please Mama."

The twins' older sister Amara, standing in the doorway, rolled her eyes, causing Rhiannon to giggle. "Amara, Mama's going to tell Flora and me about the princess again."

Amara smiled. Everything was falling into place. It was just a matter of time. The final prophecy was almost at hand. Her heart hurt that her older brother Aiden, who was now ruler of his own kingdom, and their deceased sister Bryanne could not be there. Amara could not help but be upset with her brother that he thought the birth of their new siblings was not important enough to be by their mother's side.

†

The queen ruffled Rhiannon's hair while looking at her daughter's twin. At first they were not sure she could speak. The queen's eldest daughter, Amara, had told them not to worry for Flora was just a soft-spoken soul.

When the twins had been born, Amara told her mother to name her Flora after the Goddess of Flowers. Almost from the first breath they took, Flora had let her twin, Rhiannon, take the lead.

More importantly though, Amara's vision was that Flora would protect the people when she became Queen, as was her destiny. All had great faith the small child would grow into her own and become that woman when the time was right. She would rule as her grandfather had, yet with the iron fist she inherited from her mothers.

Amara then foretold that the more vocal of her younger twin sisters would be the one to protect the lands and their people. She would use every gift given to her, whether it be with her physical presence or her grandmother's visionary powers that she would inherit when she turned sixteen. That is why she told them to name her Rhiannon after the Witch Nymph Goddess. To have two seers born into one generation was truly a miracle.

✝

All of the kingdom knew the children would live up to their names, just as Amara and her siblings had and just as her mother, the Queen of Pavlone, had by becoming the queen she was destined to be.

The queen remembered back to when she had first met the now reigning Lord. *My reigning Lord...My life...* She smiled. A single tear of happiness rolled down her cheek. *My Lord...* The thought filled her with warmth and love.

"As you wish my little ones. For my princesses Rhiannon and Flora, the tale of a princess and her pirate. Let's see, how does that story begin?" Tapping her chin, Kat pretended to think.

The twins spoke in unison, "Mama, you know how it begins. It begins with 'Once upon a time...' Remember, Mama?"

With eyes damp from unshed tears the queen started the tale she knew by heart and not just from telling it every other nightfall to their daughters. She happily told and retold the story as the love for her Lord filled her heart. She smoothed her bodice, then her skirts and laid her hands in her lap as best she could.

"Okay the Princess and the Pirate." Queen Kataryna felt a movement by the doorway, knowing, without looking, who was there. She was finally home.

✝

Her Lord's presence could be felt the moment she had stepped foot back into the palace from her long journey to visit her friends in Baul. The queen had wished to make

3

the journey herself but the timing would not allow it; she was too far along to travel safely. Especially since she had been having false pains for over a full cycle of the moon. Instead, she stayed at the palace making preparations and awaiting her return. Kataryna prayed, to all the Gods that would hear her that her Lord would return in time.

A warm loving smile engulfed the queen's features. Her Lord had made it in time; her life was now almost complete.

The queen looked down upon her twins who begged each night for the telling of the fairy tale. The tale they heard, of course, was the much edited and whimsical version.

The real version goes more like this:

Once upon a time there lived a princess named Kataryna. Her father, King Theos, ruled over Pavlone and was loved very much by his people. He wanted only for her happiness. That is why he kept her sheltered from the real world. He wanted nothing to hurt his beautiful child. He was able to keep this from happening until her fifteenth season when her pirate found her. This is their story.

Chapter One

Each king trained from birth to rule Pavlone with honor, as well as courage and love for his people. Into each generation was born a son, who in turn ruled as his father had before him. Never in the known history of the land had a daughter ruled. To even consider such a thing was cause for banishment. Through the generations, little changes took place, leading to bigger ones, like giving women the authority to own land and to even vote in elections. Anything became possible, even perhaps one day a princess being supreme ruler of all the kingdoms.

The kingdoms of Pavlone, Holan, and Salara came to be known as The Trinity. Each of the three held independent ruling parties, with Pavlone being the largest. With the abundance of wealth held in Pavlone, the other two looked there for guidance.

Over the generations, smaller kingdoms sprang to life as princes and princesses left home to seek their own lands. Leaving with them were sons and daughters of the villagers, following in hopes of opening their own shops in the new towns. Some succeeded, others perished in the harsh, new lands. Those that survived became strong and prospered under the protection of The Trinity.

Very rarely in the hundreds of generations did any of the kingdoms contemplate invading the others. Any invasions that did occur were ended quickly, easily overpowered by the king's army. As trade prospered, the royals' wealth grew. Royal heirs were born, they were promised in wedlock, never once marrying out of either the royal or nobleman bloodline.

Each new line of heirs upheld the convictions of worshipping only the old Gods. Priests from other lands would travel to The Trinity, only to be turned away at the borders. It remained as such until one hundred generations before the birth of the currently reigning King Theos.

For each of the last one hundred generations was born into every second royal generation, a seer of prophecy. The seer was always a female and told of two new Goddesses speaking to them. Those with the gift were believed to be a disciple of the Goddesses and were treated with reverence wherever they traveled.

The first seer told of a foreboding prophecy. A queen, bearing black eyes and the sweetest soul to ever have lived, would make the ultimate sacrifice. The queen was to die in childbirth bestowing unto the king a daughter. As no other child was to be born, the princess would inherit the throne. Such an action was unheard of and unfathomable. Furthermore, the prophecy foretold of a darkness falling over the lands, when the kingdoms would fall to a warlord with a dragon upon his body.

The prophecy told of the warlord destroying the royal line, reigning in the queen's place. When all was thought to be lost, she would return. She would bring with her salvation for all, ending the many seasons of war and devastation. She would restore The Trinity.

King Theos's generation was the one hundredth to have a seer born into the bloodline.

As the prophecy passed from one seer to the next, pieces were lost. Once it arrived upon the ears of Lady Bibiana all she knew of the prophecy was that darkness would descend upon their lands and all hope would be lost. If the rest of the prophecy had been known, her father would never have permitted her to marry Prince Theos.

At the wedding of Prince Theos and Lady Bibiana, the throne was passed on, crowning Theos as king. One season later, they were blessed with the birth of Princess Kataryna. As Queen Bibiana lay dying after childbirth, the Goddesses arrived to take her home.

With their arrival, they brought with them the full knowledge of the prophecy, bestowing it upon the queen. She knew then...the result of her giving birth had set the prophecy in motion. It was to be a darkness of evil, which would spread through the lands wreaking devastation as it went. The queen also knew who the She was that would come. She was beautiful with hair as black as her daughter's eyes and bearing eyes as blue as the seas. She would come from the sea, riding the waves of destiny.

The queen vowed to go peacefully if only the Goddesses would look after her daughter. If they would help her find her way when she became lost and lead her back to the woman of the sea.

They pledged to do what they could. However, the prophecy had to unfold as it had been foretold. They did not see a reason, though, why they could not nudge the young princess a little along the way.

7

As one season passed into another, the Goddesses kept watch as agreed. The child grew into a beautiful, high-spirited, stubborn young princess. With only a few sunrises left before the start of her fifteenth season, the Gods pulled the blue-eyed sea warrior in the direction of the princess. They knew doing so would bring about the deaths of many.

The Goddesses did what they must for the prophecy to be upheld; no matter the cost.

†

"I promise, Father, not to wander far. I only want to ride for a little while and will be back in time for our evening meal. You will be able to see me from your study window. I am fifteen now, so I should be allowed to leave the palace on my own. Besides there are always guards within shouting distance. Please Father." Princess Kataryna never whined nor begged her father for a thing. However, this day was different. A feeling had overcome Kat that sunrise telling her she must go riding.

King Theos loved his daughter more than anything in the known world. He could never say no to her, unless it regarded her safety. What she was asking made him wary. She wanted to go riding alone. How would she be protected? She could fall from the horse and be hurt. He did not worry about the people of his country hurting her. His subjects loved him. King Theos had always been known for paying well above what they would receive in the market for the food and materials taken from them for the palace.

Still he balked at letting her go by herself. "I am not sure. You are still so young and you are not familiar with any weapon to defend yourself. I really think Renaldo or Pelor should go with you." He picked up his goblet and drank,

8

washing down his morning meal, as well as the lump now forming in his throat.

"Father, I do so know how to defend myself. Renaldo has been teaching me how to use a sword." She knelt in front of the king her dress and petticoats flowing out around her as she did so. Kataryna hated wearing all the frilly clothes. She wished she could just wear breeches and a tunic like the men.

His heavy silver goblet landed upon the table with a thud, sending his plate skittering across the table. "What?!"

"I apologize in advance if I have caused friction between the two of you. I know that you and Renaldo love one another and I do not want to cause trouble. I must say though, Father, you have tried to keep me innocent and naïve all these years. You have kept the outside world at bay so I would not be harmed. One thing I am not though, is defenseless. I love you for doing what you thought was right. However, I feel it is time I grow up. If I am to rule in your place after you are gone, must I not be allowed to learn? You and Renaldo have done a wonderful job raising me, Father, but do you not think it is time?"

The king was speechless. His little girl was ready to fly on her own. Was he ready? Renaldo told him this day would come soon. He loved Renaldo just as he had loved Kataryna's mother, who had died in childbirth. Even with that, he was upset that Renaldo had taken it upon himself to teach her the art of defense without speaking to him first. He had wanted his little girl to be just like her mother. He had to admit that she was the spitting image of her, except for her height. Kataryna inherited that from him.

He gazed up at the queen's portrait over the fireplace, then back at his daughter. They both shared the same enchanting eyes. The eyes were what had captured him when he met her mother. He looked into eyes that were identical.

9

"Do you know how much like your mother you look? You have the same beautiful, long, color-of-the-night-sky hair, olive complexion, and your eyes…they are your mother's. They were what drew me to her. I had never seen black eyes before. When I lost her, part of me was lost also. I am thankful every day that Renaldo was there to help me back from the dark hole I fell into and to remind me that I had responsibilities. I have done the best I could. I only pray to the Gods that it has been enough."

He pulled her up into his lap, just as he had done so many times over the seasons. He noticed for the first time how much she had grown. She was no longer a small child. "I only want for your happiness, always remember that. No matter what, your happiness is most important. Is all this restlessness because of your upcoming marriage to Prince Nicholas during the winter solstice? Do you not wish to marry him?"

✝

The princess thought about her upcoming marriage. Did she really want to spend the rest of her life being a wife to a king? She thought of having only to serve him and have his children. The idea did not appeal to her. She knew there must be more to life. She wanted adventure and with marrying the prince that was not to be. The princess however did not want to disappoint her father. She especially did not want to disappoint Renaldo who had been most instrumental in arranging the marriage.

"Father, Prince Nicholas seems to be a wonderful man and I am sure he will make a good husband. I am sure he will be a great king." She tried to sound optimistic. She wanted only to please her father. She wanted him never again to know the heartache he had felt after losing her mother.

✝

He knew better. She was hiding something. King Theos could hear what she was not saying. "Kat, if you are unhappy I will stop this marriage from happening. Renaldo has been perhaps pushing a little too much. I think I will tell him to put it on hold for a season or two. I feel you should go to visit with your aunt Annessa; she is at Holan. It would be good for both of you. She is still saddened by losing her husband last season."

"I will think about it, Father. However, can I go riding? Please, Father?" When she batted her eyes the king almost always gave into her; she was his true weakness. He only prayed that one day she would not prove to be his downfall as well. Theos knew that sometimes she acted like a spoiled child. Hopefully she would outgrow it soon.

Hugging his daughter, he did what he knew he would. "Yes, you may go riding. I wish you would reconsider and at least let your bodyguard Pelor accompany you. You will not though, will you?" Knowing she would not give in, he did. In that respect, she was unlike her mother. Her mother had always known when to back down and let others rule her life; something Kataryna would never allow.

"I want you to stay within the pasture on the north side of the palace grounds."

"I will, Father. I will also take the sword I have been practicing with, and then you will maybe not worry as much."

11

†

The princess flew down the hallway, up the stairs, taking them two at a time, and down another long hallway to her rooms. Waiting for her in her outer room was Delfina, the woman who acted as her nanny, guardian, and caretaker all wrapped in one for almost all of her fifteen seasons. Her father hired her when Kataryna was two, because she was already a handful at an early age.

Kat came crashing through the door, almost knocking the poor woman over. "Slow down, child. Am I to understand the king said yes?" A grin covered her face. Delfina opened the door to Kat's bedchamber. She trailed behind the princess, picking up the clothing Kat discarded as she went. Delfina already had Kat's riding clothes laid out upon her bed.

Kat smiled at the clothes. "Planning ahead are we now, Delfina?"

Delfina had made the riding clothes special for her. She picked up what looked like a long skirt, but was actually pants. She had hated riding sidesaddle so Delfina had come up with the idea of splitting the skirt and sewing it up the middle to make pant legs. She had used enough material to make them billowy enough to look like a skirt, because no matter what she still needed to appear to be a princess.

Delfina let out a boisterous laugh. "I knew you would get your way, it was just a matter of how long it would take. Let me help you with the ties." The bodice of Kat's riding clothes was very form-fitting and tied in the back.

In no time at all, the princess was dressed and running down the back stairs on her way to the stables. She rounded the corner at full speed into the hallway leading to the kitchen and ran into Renaldo, knocking him down.

Reaching down to help him up, she was mortified at what she had done.

"Please forgive me, Renaldo. I know you have told me many times I should not be running in the palace or running at all because it is unladylike. I am very sorry." She lowered her head in embarrassment.

✝

The short balding man brushed off his breeches and straightened his tunic. "Kataryna, where are you going in such a hurry? You do not have studies today, so you are not rushing because you are late for those. So where are you going?" As always, he disguised the annoyance this child caused him by acting as if it was just fatherly concern for her. If she were not the only heir to the throne and his only chance at obtaining all the wealth of Salara when she married the prince, he would have done away with her as he had her mother.

It had been so easy for him to do. He was Queen Bibiana's brother and she was having problems giving birth. The healer needed help and the only other healer experienced enough was with the king. King Theos and his entourage had traveled to the northern region to sign a peace treaty with the king of Salara and had not yet returned. The princess had been stuck in the birth canal, so the healer had cut open the queen's belly to deliver the child. Thalia had done this many times before; she never understood why the queen died. What she had not known was while she handed the baby to one of her trainees he had slipped poison into the queen's open belly.

He asked himself once again, as he listened to the princess blabber on, why he put up with her. Ah, yes…the

13

diamonds and other precious gems of Salara that will be all mine when she marries the prince, and then she, her father, and her prince all mysteriously die. Ah and of course, at last both kingdoms will also be mine.

He noticed her attire. "Ah, going riding are we? I will meet you at the stables and be your escort for the day."

"Father said I could go alone today. I am old enough now I do not need an escort. Father also now knows I can defend myself if need be."

Renaldo looked at her in disbelief. Had she told the king he had been teaching her how to use a sword and the Far East martial art forms? He was still unsure why he gave in to her so easily and agreed to let her train. Then he remembered—he wanted to keep the little wench happy until the death that he had planned for her. He stammered on his words. "How…um…how did your father find that out?"

Her straightened posture conveyed confidence. "I told him. You know I cannot hide anything from Father. He seemed worried at first, then proud." Looking down at her brown leather riding boots Kat kicked at an imaginary pebble.

He really did not think she would tell him. She most definitely was growing up. "That is good. We do not want him to be angry with us. I, however, do not think it proper or safe for you, being the princess, to go out unchaperoned, no matter what age. I think you are being childish wanting to go alone. I will go with you." He turned and started toward the stables.

The princess ignored his insult. "No! Father said I could go alone. I am too old enough. I am fifteen seasons old. Please Renaldo, for once let me feel like I can do something on my own. You and Father have raised me properly. You also have completely sheltered me from the world. I think it is time I become a little more dependent on myself, do you not think? I will not be gone that long, or go that far, so do not worry, no harm will come to me. Please Renaldo, respect my wishes on this." She met his eyes.

As large as the part of him was that wanted the wealth and power; there was still a small part of him that did think of her as his daughter, albeit a miniscule part. "I take it this is how you talked your father into it as well? Fine…go, but I warn you, if harm comes to you, I will be first in line to scold you." He could not help himself—he smiled.

"Yes, Father saw reason just as you did. Thank you. You will not be sorry, I promise." She leaned over, kissed his cheek, and whispered to him. "Thank you, Papa." With that, she scurried down the hall, wanting to be on her way.

Calling him Papa made him smile for a brief moment. Yes, the more she liked him the better chance there was she would do exactly as he asked her, no matter her true opinion on the matter.

†

The surrounding lands of Pavlone were breathtaking. The palace itself sat atop what looked like a small mountain. The valleys were lush and green with numerous varieties of flowers and vegetation. The fields prospered for hundreds of seasons. When all were in full bloom, as they were now, it was beyond words. The villagers had made sure the beauty continued right to the port. All the homes and businesses were painted with dyes in colors to match the landscaping. Animals roamed freely, no barriers to hold them.

Not one of the other lands that bordered Pavlone compared in that respect. Two were abundant in minerals and ores, while the other was flowing with mines full of gems.

Trade worked well between all, each needing what the other had. Between them sat dense, beautiful forests, where wildlife was copious. The king assumed not one person living in his kingdom or any of the surrounding ones wanted for anything, thinking all were prosperous.

The lone dark figure sitting astride an enormous beast of a horse had come from the borderlands of the kingdoms, stealing and trading her way to Pavlone. Her goal had been to make her way to the port and steal aboard a ship, going to faraway lands. This traveler wanted to see other lands just as much as she wanted to be a pirate for the last fourteen seasons; since turning five seasons old, when she and her mother had traveled via ship across the sea to be with her father. They had encountered pirates along the way and the small child had become enamored with them.

Standing in the saddle, looking down upon the valley, something seemed out of place. There sitting on a boulder below, was a vision. Undeniably a vision in beauty, but where were her escorts? No respectable young lady would be out alone without an escort, let alone out this late in the afternoon. The sun had started to make its descent in the western sky.

The traveler's mind and hormones raged. Perhaps a handsome fee would be paid for returning the girl to her home, but of course not until the traveler had a chance to taste that beauty.

"Where is her horse, huh boy? She must have gotten out here somehow."

The rider patted the horse's neck. "I know, I know. I look like I am talking to myself again and people might think I am crazy. Luckily, there is no one around right now. It is just you and me, boy, as always. Now let us go see about little miss and why she is all alone."

†

Kataryna sat upon a small boulder in the valley resting. She rubbed her feet, trying to take some of the soreness from them. As much as it hurt to sit, her feet hurt more. She had been having a wonderful afternoon riding through the meadows. She knew she had gone farther than she agreed to, but it was such a beautiful day.

She sat replaying her stupidity in her mind. She had been starving, long since having eaten the sandwich she had brought with her. Kataryna remembered there were berry bushes on the other side of the meadow, racing across at full gallop.

It all happened in a split moment. In one breath she was riding full ahead to her goal, the next her horse was rearing up and throwing her to the ground. As she sat gathering her wits about her, it was then that she realized what had scared the horse. Kataryna watched as the snake slithered away and as her horse ran across the field in the opposite direction of the palace, leaving her behind. Carefully getting up, she brushed herself off. Knowing she would probably be walking back to the palace, she prepared herself for a scolding. They would send search parties out for her when she did not return by the time the evening meal was set on the table.

The princess sat down gingerly; every part of her body hurting. Her backside hurt from landing on it, her legs and feet from walking and her arms from…well, they just hurt as well.

She told herself she was a princess and she should not have to walk. "I should have listened to Father. I only wanted a little alone time and look at what I got instead. Ooh, Father is going to have such a fit."

The princess knew her father tried to shelter her from the world. Just as she knew he wanted her to marry the prince and not concern herself with leading the kingdom. Kataryna, however, wanted something different. She idolized her father, wanting only to follow in his footsteps. She wanted to be the first queen ruler in the history of Pavlone. However, if she married the prince, she would never have the life she wanted. She sat contemplating what she truly wanted. "If only Father would let me."

Rubbing her feet some more, she suddenly felt uneasy. Kataryna felt she was being watched, which terrified her.

"What was I thinking coming out here alone?" It was then that Kataryna saw the rider coming across the meadow toward her. The rider was dressed all in black and she feared the worst. Her mind raced with all the possibilities that someone from a faraway land had followed her and wished her harm.

Kataryna rapidly climbed down from the boulder. Snatching up her boots, she made an effort to run from the would-be attacker. Having only gone a few feet, her foot caught in a hole and down to the ground she went, taking the impact of the fall with her face. She cried out.

The rider saw her try to run and spurred the horse on. When the girl began to go down, the horse instinctively started into a full-out run. Rider and horse were too late as they both watched her hit the ground hard. The rider cringed. "Ooh, that's goin' to leave a mark."

The horse stopped beside the princess and she looked up, and up, and up some more. This horse was the largest she had ever seen in her young life. However, it was not the horse that made her heart stop. It was the rider. The first thing she saw was a black leather boot. Her eyes traveled a little further and saw black leather breeches.

The princess's mind screamed from within. *What will this barbarian do to me once he knows who I am?* She looked up from the leg to see a black tunic and a black leather vest. Then she saw a long braid down the rider's back as he dismounted. The rider lowered a glove-covered hand to help her up from the ground.

Kataryna slowly took the offered hand. A whisper of a voice in her head told her she should trust this stranger. A strong hand lifted her to a standing position. It occurred to her that he must be very strong to be able to lift her so easily from the ground. She grasped his arms and realized she was correct as she felt the muscles twitch beneath the shirt. He was most solidly built and surely not just an ordinary farmer. She thought maybe he served in her father's army or the army of a neighbor.

Once standing the rider did not let go of her as Kataryna expected, instead he put his hands on her waist. "Thank you, kind sir, for helping me up, but I..." She stopped midsentence when she heard the deep laughter come from the tall rider. That was when she realized that he towered over even her.

It was not the height that stopped her but the deep, rich laughter. It spread warmth throughout her entire body. Never before had she such a reaction. Never before had she felt so safe, at peace and just as suddenly alive and wanting to know this stranger better. Even with that, Kataryna was terrified. This brute of a man could kill her, and there was no knight to come to her rescue.

Kat thought for a moment. Did she wish to be rescued? *No!* Something in this person called to her. She brought her hand up, laying it upon her savior's chest.

"Ah!" Gasping, Kat pulled back slightly upon feeling that the chest belonged to no man but a well-formed, muscular woman. Bringing her head up, she looked into the face that rapidly warmed her heart. "Oh my..." The princess looked into eyes that had no color, the irises as clear as crystals, with the tiniest hint of blue, so pale she almost thought it her imagination. They were undoubtedly the most beautiful eyes she had ever seen. She followed the eyes to the perfectly angular nose to the strong chin. There was no doubt in her mind this was the most amazing woman she had ever seen. Kataryna found herself having trouble breathing as her heart beat faster.

Once more, Kat looked into those eyes, thinking she could see the woman's soul. Those eyes, she could get lost in them forever. For the barest moment, she thought it should bother her that the person who stirred so much in her was a woman, then without hesitation, she gave in to her heart.

Upon realizing the young woman grasped that she was a female, the rider let go of Kataryna's waist and took a step back. The beauty before the princess took her hat off, tucked it under her arm and bowed. "I am Raven, my lady, and I am at your service."

Never before had the princess acted so giddy. She extended her hand, palm down for the woman in black to kiss it. "I am Kataryna, and thank you for helping me."

Raven took the offered hand and kissed it gently, not letting go of it just yet. She looked up at eyes blacker than the night and lost her soul. "Your eyes. They are most beautiful. Never before have I seen black eyes."

Kataryna blushed, her face turning hot. She knew she should not be so forward but the words left her lips before she could stop them. "And never before have I seen mesmerizing eyes such as yours. I feel I can see into your soul if I so choose...If you so wish it." She let herself be pulled into strong arms once more. She, the princess, soon to be wed to Prince Nicholas, wanted to be in this woman's arms for all eternity.

How could that be? How could she feel what her heart was telling her for a complete stranger? A stranger that gave off an aura of a criminal. It terrified Kataryna at the same time that it enthralled her. Then she remembered her father's words. It had been her mother's eyes he had been drawn to. Now standing before her, this woman was staring into her eyes.

Kataryna smoothed a wrinkle on Raven's sleeve, once again feeling the muscular arm beneath. "So what brings you out here? Do you work for my father?"

†

Did Raven want to tell this young girl the truth, having hidden who and what she was for so long? Did she even know herself any longer? Something told her this was no mere farmer's daughter; she was so much more.

Raven surmised Kataryna was well-bred and probably one of the noblemen's daughters, therefore Raven would not be good enough for her. She felt in her heart she could not lie to her. *But why? Why can I not?* She admitted to herself that this young slip of a thing was the most heavenly creature she had ever laid eyes on.

She muttered under her breath. "Why do I feel as if I wish to remain for eternity with this young girl in my arms?

Does she have me under a spell?" Although Raven had only known her for a few moments, she was undeniably drawn to her. What remained of Raven's heart was no longer her own.

Then she realized what it was: the eyes. Raven fell into the abyss known as love, knowing she would do anything for this woman. Those same feelings in turn told her to run, run from the heartache she knew would follow.

"Actually, I was just passing through on my way to catch a ship. I do not exactly work for anyone. I make do in any little way I can." There was nothing she could do to stop the sadness from seeping into her voice. When Kataryna pulled away from her, Raven's heart hurt.

Raven sighed.

The princess shed silent tears as she turned from Raven. She let her heart rule her emotions. "Then I must stand aside and let you be on your way. I am sorry for detaining you."

Raven took her arm and turned Kataryna back to face her. She held the young girl's face in her hands as she wiped the tears away with her thumbs. "Please Kat, why do you shed tears? We do not even know each other. Alas, I am sure if you were ever to truly know me, to ever find out who I really am, you would be glad to be rid of me." Having already lost her heart to the young girl, the name Kat just rolled off her tongue, it felt right and comforting.

Kataryna tilted her head up, looking into those amazing eyes once more. "That is not true. I feel as if I have known you for many lifetimes. I feel I belong here in your arms and you in mine. I do not know why I feel this way. I do know that I like that you call me Kat." She reached up and traced a small scar on the left side of Raven's neck.

Raven had to tell her the whole truth, even if it drove her away. "Kat, I do not work for anyone else, because I am what you would call a rogue, a criminal. I have been on my own for a few seasons since my father died. He worked himself to death in the fields to feed his king. My mother killed herself after we buried him. She loved him so much she could not live without him. My family was nothing but poor farmers. Almost everything they farmed went to the palace."

Raven tried to hide her bitterness for the royal family, but failed. "I have nothing but contempt for the royal family. They are the reason my family is dead. My parents were naïve. However, the love they had for one another was worth more than anything in the world. I steal what I need and then move on. I am sure I am a wanted person in more than one town. You, on the other hand, I can tell, come from the upper class. You are probably the daughter of a nobleman. A nobleman who would no doubt put my head on a pike for a reward."

Kataryna knew what she was trying to do. Raven was trying to push her away. Even if she spoke the truth, it did not change the feeling that overwhelmed her.

Neither one of them could comprehend how they could have such feelings for one another so quickly. A nobleman's daughter? Kat's mind told her that she must tell the dark, mysterious woman the truth. Could she though? She was sure Raven would run upon hearing who she was. Why did her heart hurt so? Kat tensed in Raven's arms.

"What is it? Am I correct in guessing who you are? It is nothing to be ashamed of."

"I am not ashamed of who I am. I should have told you sooner. When I do, you will want nothing to do with me. You will hate me." The tears came again, making her feel as if she were a small child. Kat wanted to portray herself as a grown woman; a strong woman who did not become emotional at the slightest things.

"There is nothing you could say that would make me hate you, not ever. Who you are does not matter to me. Now, let us get you home before your parents get worried. We will talk along the way." She kissed Kat upon her forehead.

Kataryna smiled, even though her heart ached knowing how the truth would hurt this striking, handsome, spirited woman. There were not enough words to describe the rogue who had saved her.

†

Raven helped her onto her horse and then swung herself up behind her. Once settled behind Kataryna, she leaned forward reaching around her for the reins. Her lips were close to the smaller woman's ear. Raven had to stop herself from taking the delicate morsel between her teeth.

She was so close. Just to nibble the tender flesh there and bestow soft kisses down her neck. Her libido soared trying to take control, then, her conscious reasserted itself. Raven needed to focus on the task at hand. She needed to get the younger woman home, besides Kataryna did not need the likes of her in her life.

Sitting back on the horse, she took a deep breath, brought the wall back up and steeled her courage once more. This young Lady was too far out of reach for her. "Where to, my lady?"

†

Kataryna felt Raven physically as well as emotionally pull away from her. She knew she was not meant to feel Raven withdrawing but did nonetheless. The princess felt the wall the moment it went up. She knew why. It was quite apparent Raven disliked all the noblemen and their families. Kataryna's heart told her Raven felt herself beneath Kat's bearing.

The princess contemplated how she should word where she wanted to be taken. Kat desperately needed to tell her who she was and at the same moment terrified that when Raven found out the truth she would dump her from the horse and take off, never to be seen again. Maybe if they could ride together for a bit and get to know each other it would lessen the impact. Kataryna knew she was deluding herself but she had to try.

"I am pretty sure my father is currently at the palace." She felt Raven's body stiffen behind her. "Do not worry, you are with me. No one would dare lay a hand upon you. You will be quite safe."

✝

The thought of going to the palace horrified Raven. She did not want to be captured after coming so close to her dreams. It angered her to have to face the same people she blamed for her family's death.

She would, however, do it. Do anything, go anywhere for the beauty in her arms. Raven knew there was no length she would not go to in order to please Kataryna. Her Kat. She leaned forward once more and her lips grazed Kataryna's ear as she spoke.

"Your wish is my command," she whispered.

†

They talked as they slowly rode through the fields. They talked about mundane things, the wildlife in the area, the forest itself. Kataryna pointed out the different flowers as they went. They came across her favorites, the morning glories, which were not currently open and she told Raven all about them.

They did not speak of whom they were, where they came from, or where they were going, which suited both of them just fine for the moment.

Neither knew which brought up the subject, but they found themselves discussing weaponry. Kataryna had seen the sword that hung from Raven's hip and found it to be stunning. She would have sworn the hilt of the sword was a black panther's head. After several moments of silence, she asked, without hesitation, about the sword.

"Raven..." She squeezed the hand that at some point in their journey had made its way around her waist to rest itself on her belly.

Raven squeezed the hand back. "Yes Kat..."

It warmed her inside to hear how her name rolled from Raven's mouth. Raven was the only person, other than her father, to call her Kat. She liked it very much. "Your sword is so unique. Who made it? Is that a black panther on the hilt of it? Where did you learn to use it? Is it heavy? What are the jewels? How long did it take to make it?" She prayed she was not overstepping herself as she rattled the questions off so fast that they left her out of breath. She felt Raven's body shake with laughter behind her.

"Slow down, little one, and breathe..."

"Sorry..."

Raven squeezed the smaller hand once more. "Never be sorry for asking what is on your mind, just remember to breathe in between questions." She felt Kataryna nod. "Okay…yes it is a black panther. As for who made it, I did." She left it at that not wanting to tell her more. This, after all, was a well-bred young lady and not one of the barmaids she was used to keeping company with.

Kataryna could not leave it alone though. She found it inspiring that Raven would be able to make such a masterpiece. "Wow! You made it. It is amazing. How though, who taught you the art of folding steel? You did not say how long it took to make. Have you made others?"

"What did I say about breathing? You are going to cause yourself harm if you keep that up. Yes, I made it. As for who taught me, that is a bit more complicated. It took quite some time to make." She did not elaborate, trying to buy herself some time. She knew Kat would ask, but did not know if she could bring herself to tell the story.

†

This time Kataryna missed the body language that would have told her to stop and not push the issue. Instead, she pushed and asked her again. It was then that she felt Raven withdraw and Kataryna suddenly became cold. She shivered as she felt dread come over her.

Raven brought the horse to a stop, withdrew her arm from around Kataryna, resting her hands on her own thighs. So lost in thought, Raven did not notice that Kataryna had managed to turn herself partially around on the horse so that she now faced Raven.

Kataryna took Raven's hands in hers, holding them in her lap. She waited a few more moments. Realizing Raven's mind was elsewhere, possibly reliving some terrible torment, she became worried. Kataryna's heart told her what Raven needed to hear, to bring her back from her torment.

"Please come back to me, my love. Whatever it is, I am here. I am here for you, to help you face anything." Gently she laid her hand upon Raven's cheek. Raven felt ice cold; Kataryna was terrified. She brought her other hand up to Raven's face. Both of Raven's hands instinctively went to Kat's thighs and held on, her fingers digging into her flesh, causing Kat to flinch in pain. Raven's hands tightened. It was as if life itself depended upon the connection between the two of them.

Holding Raven's face in her hands, she stroked her cheeks with her thumbs. "Please Raven, come back to me, I need you. I cannot make it home without you. I need the safety only you can provide. I need your protection in body and soul. Please..."

The words were out before she thought about what she was saying. She realized she was lucky, though, in that Raven did not comprehend what she had said. She just hoped they would not attach themselves to her subconscious mind. Her instinct told her never to show weakness where Raven was concerned.

When Raven still did not respond, Kat found herself doing the one thing she truly hoped would bring this dark, spirited woman back to her; listening once more to her heart she kissed her. It was so gentle that she was not sure if their lips had truly met. Looking into Raven's eyes, she saw the fire. Kataryna knew it had worked. Raven was back.

"I am sorry; I did not know what to do. I was terrified for you. I am sorry if I offended you." Kataryna's hands moved from her face down to rest on Raven's thighs.

†

Raven felt herself coming back into her body as Kataryna's lips touched her own. At first, she was unsure if it had happened or if she were dreaming. Looking down she felt herself falling into Kataryna's eyes once more. It was then that she knew…their lips had touched and if she were to die now she would die happy.

"Do not be sorry. Did you follow your heart?" Raven laid her hand upon Kat's wrist. She could feel the young girl's rapidly thudding pulse under her fingertips.

"Yes."

"Then that is all that matters. Remember to follow your heart. It will lead you home where you belong. Anything else will always be lies." It was in that moment Raven knew she would forever belong to this creature here in her presence, no matter what was to come.

Kataryna's heart then led her further than she dared to go. "Home with you."

As one's heart swelled, the other's broke.

Raven knew it could never be. "You are young, beautiful and precious. I am sure there is a prince or two fighting for your hand. I could never give you what they…" Kat's face transformed and Raven saw fear. Her heart saddened. Her mind rebelled and raced down a path she did not want to tread. So there was a prince waiting for Kataryna. She should have known. Raven heaved a heavy sigh, feeling a tightening in her chest. Taking Kat's hands in hers, Raven brought them up to lie on her chest. "Kat, as I said, you are most precious. I can tell you have lived a sheltered life, which has left you very naïve. This is not a bad thing though." Raven saw the defiant look on her face and chuckled.

"Do not give me that look. Knowing how to use a sword does not make you worldly. What I am…"

"And Raven, what you are? Is that what you are trying to tell me? That it is I who is not good enough for you?" Anger flared in Kat's voice.

Raven recoiled at the thought that Kataryna felt herself unworthy. "No, that is not at all what I meant. If you would stop interrupting me for a moment please, I could finish." Silence fell briefly.

"Now as I was saying…where was I?" Raven thought for a moment. She ran a hand over her face as if to clear her mind. "Ah yes. I am very glad you can defend yourself. There is, however, more to the world than that. I am positive you have never traveled, truly traveled and lived among the people of this land. You have lived a very pampered life. This can be a good thing though. You will make him a caring, loving wife and a wonderful mother to his children. All the things I could never be to anyone. Do you understand what I am saying?"

†

Kataryna could not stop the tears from flowing, nor did she care to. The tears showed her grief at the truth Raven had spoken. That same grief helped to control the anger she felt at having no control over her own destiny.

Why could she not choose who shared her life? Why could she not be with her? She knew the answer, because she was the princess and future queen of this kingdom. Because she was born into the wrong family. What if she were to just disappear with Raven? It would be so simple to get onto the ship with her and go to wherever it leads. They could start a new life together.

Kataryna tilted her head up to look into those mesmerizing eyes and she knew she could not. Her future was already laid out for her; yet her rebellious streak continued. "Yes, I understand what you are saying. It is true, all of it. My future is not my own, everything has already been decided by my father and uncle. What if it is not what I want though? What if I want something different for myself? I am fifteen summers old now; I can decide things on my own."

Raven drew back from Kataryna. "No! You are a noblewoman. You will marry a prince and be a princess. It is what you were born to be, in that there is no doubt. You are too dignified and far too special to be with a mere peasant." Raven lowered her head as the words caught in her throat but they had to be expressed. "Especially a peasant and criminal like me. I would bring you nothing more than heartache. I could never provide for you as you are accustomed to." Kat's face scrunched a bit. "I see the little wheels turning in that pretty head of yours, my Kat, what are you thinking?"

Kataryna's mind was whirling around the possibilities. She unfortunately did not stop to think for a moment before blurting out her thoughts. "You are very good with a sword, what if you were to be appointed as a guardian to the princess."

†

It was now Raven's turn to look horrified. Her soul, spirit, mind, and heart all screamed at once, almost causing her to fall from her horse. *THE PRINCESS?!* No! It could not be! She could not be *The Princess*.

31

Raven felt the world collapsing around her. How could this be? For the first time in so long she had felt a moment of happiness only to have it ripped from her hands by the Fates. At first, she thought she had misheard the young girl, and then she knew she had not when she saw the look upon the princess's face. Raven's world did then come crashing down upon her head.

"NO!"

Chapter Two

As if knowing of the storm that was brewing between the women, the forest became unearthly quiet. Birds stopped their singing while all other animals ceased movement. They felt the air sizzling with electricity from emotions that were ready to boil over.

Raven felt rather than heard the quietness of the forest and immediately knew it was not a good sign. She knew this stillness meant foreboding and dread circled her heart. She had just met this beautiful woman who had immediately captured her heart. That same heart now told her to run, run as fast as she could, for it was about to be broken.

Kataryna sobbed uncontrollably. Through hiccups she told Raven who she was. "You will hate me, I know you will." The princess wiped her face on her sleeve.

"Kat, tell me what you need to." The dread that had been circling her heart now firmly imbedded itself. Kat looked to Raven as if she were trying to gather her courage.

"My father is King Theos, I am Princess Kataryna."

Raven let go of her, vaulted from her horse, landed in a crouching position ready to fight. Anger contorted her face and instinct took over. "So where are your guards, surely they would not let you out of the palace on your own." She looked around, fear running through her.

"Please Raven...let me explain..." Kataryna slid from the horse.

She backed farther away from the princess, stumbling as if dealt a heavy blow. Raven's insides were turning to ice. She had fallen for the king's daughter. Fate had once more laughed at her. "I see. I sincerely hope you had a good laugh when I told you of my family." She looked around for the guards, the anger filling her.

"Please...I would never laugh at you nor your family. Please believe that. I am so sorry for your loss. Can you not forget who I am? Can I not just be Kat? Kataryna, your Kat. Please?" She took Raven's hands in hers, trying to hold on for dear life.

Raven pulled her hands away from Kataryna as if her touch burned. "I cannot, I too am sorry. Sorry for who you are. Now where are your guards?" She turned to mount her horse, needing to get far away from this woman as fast as she could.

Kataryna had to stop her, had to make her understand. "I begged my father to let me come alone. I promised him not to go too far. Then my horse took off and dumped me on the ground. Please do not leave. Please...I...I care...if you care about me you will not leave me here."

Raven stood by her horse, laughing. It, however, was not a kind laugh. It was cruel and cutting. "Care about you? What a farce! Do you think me that stupid? I remember my place, Princess; you would do well to remember yours. I am nothing more than mere trash to the likes of you. I am not even fit to be in your presence. Here, my Princess, let me help you up, you cannot be found walking back to the palace.

Just as I cannot be found riding with you on the same horse, so I shall walk."

She roughly grabbed the princess by the arm and shoved her onto the horse. Kataryna's sobbing began anew. Raven herself did nothing to stop the tears as they streamed down her face as well. She felt a fool and anger welled beyond her control inside of her. She wanted Kataryna to hurt as much as she was hurting. If Raven told her some of what she had to endure since her parents' deaths, it might give the princess a clue.

"So let us see, where was I in my telling you of my life. Ah yes, the sword...my father worked from sunup till sundown and for what? Every season when the crops were harvested guards from the palace would swoop in and take everything. We were not compensated for what was taken, they left us with nothing!

"The guards would tell him every season that he grew the best vegetables in all the lands and that he should be proud they were being taken to the palace. Father managed to hide what little he could, but it was never enough. Every season after they took the crops, he would try to find what little work there was in the village or palace to obtain what little more he could. So, you see he worked himself to death, all for your precious royal palate.

"When my father died, the fields obviously could not take care of themselves. It was harvest time so I tried my best to tend to them and Mother at the same time. Mother refused to get out of bed or eat. She died within five nightfalls after burying Father. The grief was too much for her, it killed her; as sure as if it was a dagger she used. It was then that I knew there was nothing I could do. There was no money, so I could not leave. I had to find a way to survive. The local blacksmith hated being a blacksmith and wanted to be a

35

farmer so I sold him the land, and told him I also wanted a sword in the deal.

"He told me he would teach me how to make one myself and how to use it. Over the next several moons, he did just that. I, however, too late came to realize he also drank too much and had other things in mind. He had yet to teach me how to use the sword, and he, of course, was the best swordsman around. I had no choice but to give him what he wanted in return. Yes, Princess, he took something from me that first night. It is not exactly what you think, though. When he was sober enough, he made me get on my knees to satisfy him by sucking on his manhood." She looked up at Kat sitting on the horse and saw a look of revulsion flicker across the princess's face.

"Some of us have to do disgusting things to survive, Princess, never forget that. He taught me very well how to handle my weapon, which in the end would be his undoing. Anyway, I was ready to leave. I had my bedroll and what clothes I had to my name on my horse. I went to the barn to leave and found him there. He told me I was his property and I was going nowhere." Raven's hands clenched into fists as she remembered that morning. It was more than venom that seeped into her words. It was death and destruction itself that clouded the words.

"He stood between my horse and me, not having drawn his weapon. Instead, the pig planned to show me whom I belonged to. It was so sudden, he caught me off guard. That man was the last person to ever catch me off guard and none ever will again. He knocked me down before I knew it and kicked me several times, ripping my clothes from me. He tried to hold me to the ground while pulling his own pants off but could not. I took that as my opportunity to try to get away. I got on my hands and knees, attempting to crawl away. Every part of my body hurt so I could not move very fast." Raven found herself back in a time of revulsion and fighting for her life.

Closing her eyes Raven could smell the pungent straw around her. She remembered the smell of the manure that she was sure was now on her breeches as she tried to crawl away. Raven could still feel the fear that coursed through her as she had willed her body into motion that day so long ago, as she had pushed through the pain that seared into her bones from his brutal attack. Remembering the event caused Raven to once more be able to feel his weight on top of her.

"Once again I was crawling away when I felt him on me. He had his hands on me spreading my legs apart. Then he...he had his hands on my backside. He lifted my backside up as he pulled apart and exposed where no one was permitted to touch. He tried to...I lost all reason then. I kicked back with what strength I had left. I was able to knock him off balance. I rolled over then, kicked him in his manhood.

"As he was rolling around bellowing, I retrieved his sword and drove it through him. I pulled my clothes back together as best I could and left, never looking back once. That was several seasons ago. I have learned much over that time. I learned that anything can and will be bartered for no matter what the true cost is; even one's soul and life can be traded. So now you know what I am, as I know who you are."

Raven's mind took her back all those seasons and brought her torment fresh to her mind, body, and soul. She clenched the reins tightly as she walked. After some time, Kat's voice was finally able to cut through the anger in her and bring her back to the present.

†

"I cannot help who I am or what family I was born into. I, however, will not be held responsible for such accusations. My father and uncle are good men who would not condone such abuse. I will speak with them about this, surely they will tell you the same. It had to have been rogue guards. Why did you not report this to the palace?" Kataryna's mind was racing. She was angered that such a thing would have befallen this woman and her family. Raven's malicious laughter filled her ears.

"Do you think, Princess, that my father did not do just that? He returned home beaten within a hair of death. It took him many, many sunrises to recover. Believe me, Princess, the guards were not acting on their own; they were doing what they were told. So you see, I have no use for anything or anyone that comes from the palace."

Kataryna could see the palace grounds in the distance and knew their time was almost up. She needed to make Raven understand that this was not who she was, that she was so much more. She was the princess yes, but also a woman with a heart. Timidly Kataryna asked, "Does that include me that you have no use for?"

†

Raven also saw the grounds and pulled the reins for Lyhawk to stop. Part of her wanted to go no further, while the other half wanted it to be known that it was she who returned the princess to the palace unharmed. That it was she who rescued her. "I am sorry, what were you saying, Princess?" Raven heard desperation in Kat's voice.

38

"You heard me. Look into my eyes and tell me you have no use for me. Tell me you feel nothing for me. I know you do. I felt it when we rode together and you held me. I know I did. Look at me and tell me differently."

Still facing away from her Raven answered, "I cannot."

Kataryna slid down from the horse. "Please…I cannot leave it like this between us."

The princess pulled on Raven's arm, turning her around so they stood facing each other. Raven lowered her eyes. Doing as requested, she found herself falling once more. She wanted to throw herself at this heavenly creature's feet…to beg her for forgiveness. Then she remembered once more who Kataryna was. "You are the princess and I am a murderer. That is who we are. That is what I know. It cannot be changed, ever. Therefore, we part ways here. You will be able to make it to the palace from here on your own, my princess." Raven bowed and mounted her horse.

"You told me to always follow my heart and that is what I am going to do. What I know is you are blaming me for something I had nothing to do with, something that was out of my control. You deny what is in your heart because of it. That I cannot nor will I stand for. You say you cannot because I am the princess. Fine, then I will come with you. I will denounce who I am. I will be nothing more than your Kataryna."

"My, my, my, you are feisty and outspoken for a princess. Are you not taught manners? Not to ever fight back?" Raven saw fire blazing in Kataryna's attitude.

"My father taught me to fight for what I want."

Raven stilled her antsy horse, thinking, feeling, about what Kataryna had spoken. Could she deny what she felt? On the other hand, was this a trap to capture her? No, she knew that was not the case. Kataryna was too naïve for such a thing.

"Kataryna, do you speak from the heart? Do you truly? If you..." It was then she saw them. A dozen or so men on horseback racing toward them at full gallop.

The princess looked up at the taller woman, unaware of the men charging toward them, "If I what?"

†

Kataryna saw the pain spread across Raven's features. It was then she realized Raven was not looking at her, but behind her.

As she turned to see what Raven was looking at, she heard the hoofbeats. Behind her, she heard Raven's feet hit the ground beneath them. She knew who was in the lead; it was Pelor. He would be furious. She turned back to Raven, just as Raven spun her around to put herself between the princess and the men. "No! Please Raven, we have time. We can leave here, go to the docks just as you wanted. Please, for me."

†

Raven lowered her eyes. "No, we cannot. You are who you are and I am who I am. I suppose it will be the gallows for me now." Raven now knew who the approaching men were, just as she knew there was no escape.

"No, I would never tell them who you are. Do you think so little of me?" Tears graced the princess's face.

She could not believe this was happening. Raven had been so close to leaving this country, to escaping her past. It

40

would have been so easy to do. Just get on the ship, sail away, and never look back to the hell her life had been. Raven looked back down. "Kat I..." She needed to tell her. To tell her how she felt. "I..." The men were upon them and Raven found a sword at her throat.

†

"My good man, slowly take your hands off the princess and do not think of drawing your sword. If you try, it will be the last thing you do." Pelor motioned for the other guards to watch the stranger while he moved around to swoop up the princess onto his horse.

As he maneuvered his horse around the stranger, removing his sword from the stranger's throat to be replaced by another's, it was then that he saw it was not a man, but was indeed a woman with the princess. "What in..." Wanting to pull the princess onto his horse was shortly forgotten about. Before he knew what happened, Kataryna flew into a rage. He knew her temper well, being on the receiving end of it several times.

"Pelor, how dare you assume I am in harm's way. How dare you! If you do not release her immediately, you will be very sorry. You should be thankful that she found me when she did. That beast of my horse threw me and I hurt my ankle so I could not walk back here."

Kataryna reached over, pushing the sword away from Raven. She then stood between Raven and her own bodyguard. "If you wish to do her harm, you will have to go through me to do so." Kat looked up at Raven and smiled. "Now, shall we get back to the palace, we happen to be starving and thirsty. Please send someone ahead to announce us. Have Delfina draw each of us a hot bath and have food

41

prepared." At that, she turned to Raven, "Would you please be so kind as to help me up?"

Raven understood then that this man, or anyone else for that matter, was way out of his league and would never win with this woman. Of course, neither would she and yet that thought did not bother her. She mused that Kataryna was most definitely one to be reckoned with when her ire was up. She bowed and tried to hide her laughter. "Yes, my princess, as you command."

†

King Theos and Renaldo tried their best to retrieve the story of what happened from Kataryna but she steadfastly refused to tell them a thing until she was ready. Once she had a nice hot bath and her fill of food and drink, she told them the tale. Looking across the room at Raven, who was feeling more than a little out of place, she smiled. Raven could see the candlelight in Kat's eyes and smiled back.

They had retired to her father's den after the evening meal. It was there that the story unfolded. When Kataryna finished she sensed that Renaldo did not share her father's feeling of gratitude toward Raven. Since arriving back at the palace, Renaldo had treated Raven as if she was beneath them. As they sat sipping their brandy, Kat spied on Raven over the top of her glass. Raven looked as if she were ready to bolt from the room.

Kataryna was not the only one to notice. The king had been watching Raven all evening. He knew the look, having had the same look once in his own life. It had been when he was courting Kat's mother. It was a look of pure fear, except when Raven's eyes would fall upon his daughter, then there was nothing but love showing at that moment in

42

time. When she was not gazing at Kataryna, Raven kept looking at the door as if trying to find an escape.

He feared for his daughter. She was the princess, the future queen. Kataryna had been taught to do what was best for her country, as had he. He then chanced a glance at Renaldo. He had seen that look before as well. It was a look of hatred.

Renaldo felt Theos's eyes on him. He changed his expression rapidly knowing the king would be able to read the unguarded hatred upon his face. Renaldo tried to draw from Raven where she was from. The only thing she would tell him was 'the north.' The fact that Raven wanted him to know nothing about her proved to Renaldo that she did not trust him.

"Father, I am very tired and I am sure Raven is also. So if you will excuse us, I will escort her back to her room for the night." The princess motioned for Raven to follow.

†

Once in the hall Raven let herself relax. "Thank you, Princess, I am rather tired."

"We are alone you know." Kataryna stopped so she could look up at Raven.

Raven took a step back to put some distance between them. "I am fully aware that we are alone. You, however, are still the princess. Furthermore, your guards or Renaldo not being here does not change that."

Kat's deep breath showed her frustration. "I thought maybe we had gotten past that. Hoping maybe you saw more to me than just my being the princess. Father likes you, that much I do know. I do not know what is going on with Renaldo. He usually is not so rude." Kat took a deep breath, truly puzzled by Renaldo's behavior. "Ooh…where was I…ah yes, why have you become so distant? Have I done something to offend you? Or is it just that I am the princess and you are afraid of me?"

Raven scowled at her, put her hands on Kat's hips and pulled her close. "I am afraid of no woman. That, however, does not change the most important thing." She found her hand moving with a mind of its own, caressing Kat's face.

Kat leaned into the touch. "What, pray tell, would that be?" She looked up at the answer written in Raven's eyes.

"You are still the princess and I am still a murderer." Raven let go of her, opened the door to her room and closed it behind her. She leaned against the door, then slid to the floor and let the tears flow. Screaming at herself that she should never have gone near the girl. She should have turned her horse and rode away.

The closed door did not deter Kataryna. She spoke loudly, so Raven could hear her on the other side. "Fear not, Raven, we will continue this in the morning. You know full well where my heart lies and I always get my way, my love."

✝

Kataryna's rooms were across the hall. She opened the door and walked into her sitting chamber. Delfina had lit only a few candles, assuming that Kataryna would retire to her bedchamber for the night. She crossed the room and was about to open the bedchamber door when a knock came on her outer one.

She rushed across the room and threw open the door, hoping to see Raven standing before her. Instead, she found

44

her father. "Oh, hello Father." Kat tried to hide the disappointment. "I was just going to retire for the night."

"I wanted to talk to you for a moment." The princess's red face did not go unnoticed by the king.

"I am sorry, Father. Please come in and sit by the fire." She linked her arm through his and guided him to a chair in front of the fireplace. She sat on the floor at his feet as he settled into the chair.

"Who were you hoping to find at the door, little one? Raven perhaps? You seem quite fond of her. She is interesting, I must say. Did you talk of anything special?" He feared the answers, yet he needed to know.

Kataryna thought about what to say to her father. Did she tell him the truth? Did she tell him who Raven was? She could not; she did not want to endanger Raven. Even as she decided on the middle ground, she could feel her anger flaring as she thought of what Raven had told her. She knew now was not the time to bring the matter to her father's attention. It was better saved for later, after he knew Raven better.

"Her parents were farmers. She told me about her father and the crops he grew. Raven lost both of her parents several seasons ago and has been on her own since. You should have seen her, Father. Before she knew they were guards from the palace, she put herself between them and me. Then when Pelor put his sword to her throat, she never flinched, never backed down. She was amazing..." Catching herself, she stopped midsentence.

Theos chuckled. "It sounds to me she made quite an impression. Let me tell you of what I see. I see a young, naïve girl finding love for the very first time in a somewhat roguish woman." Kataryna started to interrupt him. He held his hand up to stop her.

45

"Ah…give me a chance to finish, little one. You are so much like your mother it terrifies me. She met someone and fell in love at the same age as you are now. Alas, he was driven away by her father and the young man was never seen again. You see, she was already promised to a young prince and your Raven holds the same qualities. Young, brash, irresponsible, always in trouble and a bit of a rogue. Does that sound like her, Kat?"

Kat nodded in agreement.

"Wondering whom I am speaking of? I am speaking of myself. Yes, little one…that was I when I was younger. We married at our fathers' requests and your mother came to love and respect me. I looked at Raven this evening and saw myself. I also saw how she looked at you. I find myself liking your Raven. Do you feel the same as she?" He looked into her eyes and saw nothing but love.

"Yes, Father, but it cannot be. She will not let it." Her tears fell silently.

"Ah, I see. She sees only a princess, not what is beneath, am I correct? Hmm…do you wish to change that my child? What does your heart tell you?" He reached down, pulling her hair back from her face.

Her head bowed, unable to look up at her father. "I love her, Father, with all that I am. There are many complications, though, and she will leave tomorrow unless I somehow can stop her."

"I had no choice in the matter of who I wed. However, we were lucky we grew to love one another. What does your heart tell you?" He knew already that she was lost.

She sighed. "It tells me not to let her go. Father, my heart hurts so much at just the thought of her leaving. I want to make her stay. I know I cannot though. To force her to stay…I fear she would hate me. What do I do, Father? Please, you have to tell me what I need to do."

"Oh child, I cannot do that. I know there are things you have not told me about her. It is for you to decide. I have always instilled in you to follow your heart. In this case, it may not be the best answer. It is for the two of you to decide together, it affects her future as much as yours. You must remember one thing. You are the future Queen of Pavlone. Would she be able to accept that?"

From just the few moments Theos spent with Raven he knew she could not, at least not at this point in her life.

When his daughter had arrived back at the castle with Raven in tow, King Theos had Pelor find out all he could about the woman with his daughter. Moments before when Pelor reported to him the few fragments he was able to obtain from the guards, who had recently come from the same region as Raven, the king feared for his daughter's heart. Knowing his own daughter as well as he did, she was naïve when it came to matters of the heart.

It would have to be for the two of them to decide the course their future would take. He thought back to his own youth. His father had given him no choice in who he was to marry. What would have happened if she had not grown to love him? They both would have been miserable. His future could have turned out so differently in the blink of an eye. He was grateful that it had not. He, however, was not sure about his heir's future.

"Kat, you must not think only of yourself. You must think of Raven, and of your people, even though you are only the princess now, you must still think of them. Do not worry. She was acting in self-defense when she took that man's life. I like to think I am a compassionate King so she will not be arrested and sent to the gallows. I do not think at this time in her life being here in the palace would make her happy. Yes, she would be happy courting you, as long as she was not reminded of who you are and who you are to become. You are the princess and that will not change."

†

Kataryna sat at her father's feet watching the dying embers of the fire, never really feeling the heat that emanated from the hearth. She thought on all her father had told her. She knew she must think of the people of the kingdom, her future people. However, her mind kept returning to Raven. Could she see a future without her in it? Since birth she had been instilled with the knowledge that her people must always come first. Could she do that now? Put them before her heart? She knew the answer and it shattered her.

After some time, the words flowed quietly from within her. "What am I to do? I fear I will be lost if she leaves. I fear the people would never accept her as my consort and future wife. Must I think of them and not Raven first? Cannot I think of what I want, Father? I fear I will die without her. I could make her happy here, I could make her see reason, could I not, Father?" She knew no answer would be forthcoming. Silence hung between them.

Kataryna resigned herself to what had to be. Just as she knew she could not force Raven to stay. "There is no choice but to marry Prince Nicholas as planned, is there? Did I ever have a choice? Being born a princess, my destiny was decided at birth. I must do what is expected of me and bury what I feel in my heart. Mustn't I, Father?" She looked up into her father's eyes and saw her own sadness reflected back at her.

"If that is what you wish, child. Please take the night and think on it before you decide. Remember, it is not just your feelings you must consider. For the first time in your life you must put others first, not yourself." He stood and left her chambers, leaving her to grieve for what could not be.

Sometime after King Theos left and the fire was nothing more than ash, she stood, slowly making her way to bed. Her mind made up on what was to be done. Her heart grew heavy. Could she walk away from everything she had known since the day she was brought into this world? Yet, could she not? Could she let go of the woman who had stolen her soul? "I will be as strong as you, Father. I will do what is in my heart." Her mind made up, she fell into a fitful sleep.

†

As the king was entering his daughter's chamber to speak to her, another had been lurking farther down the hall. He had been waiting all evening to speak with Raven alone. He must make her come to understand she could not, and would not, be allowed to stay; that she was not good enough for the princess. He would wait until the king left Kataryna's chamber then knock on Raven's door. That way there was a possibility she would hear the princess's door opening and closing. This would only help in Renaldo's plan if she thought he had just come from Kataryna's chambers.

Renaldo had always been jealous of his sister Bibiana. She had married Theos and became queen, while he was expected to be only her guardian and watch over her as long as she lived. So, he in turn made sure she did not live long. He wanted it all. Renaldo wanted to be king. He would do anything to achieve his goal.

49

The wealth and power was to be his and he would do anything to ensure that happened. Kataryna was to marry the prince, pure and simple. Once they were married and suitable time would pass, then an accident would occur. He, along with the king, would play the part of the grieving fathers. Then of course, the king would be so devastated that he would take poison and die shortly thereafter, leaving him, Renaldo, to rule as king over the lands.

The power he would hold as king over both kingdoms would be backed up by the wealth of the gem and ore mines he would also obtain. He would let his power be known as he ventured forth to claim other lands in the name of Pavlone. In his mind Renaldo had it all worked out. This was just a mere obstacle to overcome by doing the only thing he knew how to do. He would intimidate this Raven into leaving.

He was also afraid Raven would tell the king how his loyal soldiers plundered the outlying countryside in the name of the king. Renaldo knew of her shortly after arriving at the palace when one of the soldiers had informed him of who she was. It would not bode well for him if the king were to find out at this point. He was confident he could cover it up, but there was always the off chance that Theos would believe the peasant.

When Kataryna opened her door and the king left, Renaldo moved from the shadows and knocked quietly on Raven's door.

†

Raven was very puzzled upon opening her door to find Renaldo standing there and not Kataryna, as she had expected. She wanted so much to go to her, to tell her they could leave together in the morning, yet knew she could not.

She fought an internal battle and was losing ground every moment. Her heart had all but won the war over her mind when the knock came. She leapt from the chair in front of the fire, knowing it was Kat at the door. Then, much to her surprise, it was not.

"May I come in, Raven? I feel we must discuss the princess." Not waiting for a reply, he elbowed past Raven into her room.

His rude behavior by entering her room without permission stunned Raven. "Excuse me, sir. I thought it was proper etiquette to wait until one was invited into a lady's room?" She stealthily closed the door behind him.

"Please, Raven, we both know you are no lady. The only true *lady* in the palace is the princess. I am sorry if I sound disrespectful. I have just come from meeting with Kataryna and King Theos. I have been elected to speak with you and am truly sorry for what I have to tell you. Please, let us sit." He motioned to the chairs in front of the fire.

Raven sat, a sense of dread encompassed her. Fear seeped into her, into her bones. She knew what he was here to tell her. The king wanted her out of the palace. She could feel it, deep inside. She however, was not prepared, for what Renaldo went on to tell her.

Renaldo needed to reel her into his grasp, so he did what he was best at, spun a web of lies and deceit. He used what his loyal-to-him-only guards had told him. Knowing Theos was a lenient and good king and would not arrest her for killing the man in self-defense, Renaldo would use the knowledge of the murder against her. "I know of no other way than to just tell you. I know it will hurt you deeply and for that I am sorry. I truly like you. I know you have had a hard life. Several moons ago one of my guards found out what happened in your region. I will make a promise to you to investigate what happened with your father's crops. That, however, is not the matter at hand. I have come with a message from Kataryna. She is sorry for misleading you. She tells me she was terrified that you would harm her, that you had already murdered someone." The look of fear on Raven's face told him he had her in his grasp.

"I do not judge you, nor will I ever speak of who you are. She is to marry Prince Nicholas. She knows that you could never provide for her. I am sorry. I know what it is like to love and not have. I was in love with Theos from the moment I met him before he married my sister, but I knew it was not to be. Then our paths crossed once more when my sister passed on. The Fates smiled on me that day. Perhaps they will smile on you too someday. I know your heart must be hurting. In time, it will lessen. I have learned that you were on your way to the docks when you happened upon Kataryna. I inquired and all of the ships are still at the docks, but will be leaving at first light." A pouch appeared from inside his tunic.

Raven was too shocked to speak as she sat and watched Renaldo pull a money pouch out. At seeing the money, anger swelled within her. Was he going to try to buy her off?

Renaldo pretended to contemplate the pouch in his hands. He felt doing this made him look pensive and that it would help to make Raven believe his lies. "I know this might offend you, but please do not let it; it is only a little that I have saved over the last couple of seasons. I want you to have it. Theos knows nothing of the money, please do not let him find out. This is the only way I could think of to compensate you for your grief. Unless there is something else I can do for you. When you decide what you wish to do please send someone to find me."

Renaldo stood, starting for the door, only to throw another sympathetic line her way before departing. "Raven, from the deepest part of my heart I am sorry. Kataryna is but a mere child and sometimes can act like one with no regard for the feelings of others. For that I must apologize. Her father and I apparently have coddled her for far too long."

As he reached for the door, Raven called his name. "Renaldo, thank you for being honest with me. I did not think you liked me. My opinion has changed. You also have my deepest sympathy that it has to be you to do someone else's dirty work for them. I do not know how but I will repay you tenfold someday for not only the money but for the courage you have shown. Once again thank you. I shall take my leave of the palace once everyone has settled for the night. Please tell *The Princess* her message has been received." She heard the door close quietly with a whooshing sound. The same sound her heart now made as it turned black as coal.

✝

Renaldo escorted her to the docks a short time later under the pretense of wanting to make sure she got there safely without being hassled by any of the guards.

A plan had already formulated in her cold heart upon seeing the pot-bellied, lazy captain. The captain leered at Raven, causing the hair to stand up on her arms. She had met another like him before and she had ended up killing him. Raven was not about to let that stop her though. If he held true to being the type of scum she thought he was it would make it even easier than she thought, especially if he tried to have his way with her. No matter though, either way his life was forfeit and her destiny was in her own hands. Any

53

humanity Raven had was lost, knowing it would not be hard to take over his ship and make it hers. She would just toss his body overboard and do the same with anyone who opposed her. The seas would be hers as well as the wealth that came with it.

A black-hearted pirate was born that day and she had her ship. The Fates no longer controlled her destiny. Raven would set about to make her own. As she cut a path through the seas, she left behind her a trail of blood and sunken ships.

Captain Raven preyed on all that crossed her path. Leaving few souls alive in her wake, she told them to spread the word. Cross her path and meet your fate.

Chapter Three

Three mornings after Raven's departure, noblemen and women arrived from every surrounding land. Lady Annessa even came out of her seclusion for the happy event. King Theos knew a mistake was being made, but he could not interfere with the chain of events already set in motion. His daughter, his only heir, was married on the fourth sunrise after Raven's disappearance. He knew she did not love him, only marrying because it was expected of her.

Kataryna came to him the night after Raven's departure, demanding the wedding take place in four sunrises, then secluded herself in her rooms. King Theos knew whom she truly loved, just as he knew his daughter had decided to leave with Raven. It broke his heart to think she was so willing to leave her home, but he did advise the princess to follow her heart.

After the disappearance of Raven, his daughter changed. She no longer was the naïve, sweet young girl that left that fateful morning to go riding. She no longer sat for hours at her father's side, giggling and laughing at his jokes. No longer did she play jokes on him, then run away leaving laughter in her wake.

King Theos assumed Kataryna spent from sunrise to sunset learning all she could about the many aspects of being a queen, of being a ruler. In actuality, she spent most of the day learning all the facets of battle. She learned how to handle her sword as a warrior would, then two swords. Then how to use throwing knives and any other item that could be used as a weapon. She found the prospect that even a teacup could be lethal, inspiring.

Renaldo, Pelor, and several others loyal to them taught her everything they knew. The two men saw the overnight change in the princess but wisely kept it to themselves. Renaldo did not want Theos upset, so he went on as if nothing had changed. Pelor knew it was not his place to question her, even though they had grown up together. He would stand by her in whatever the future held.

Her carefree nature had been shattered that morning upon finding Raven's room empty, the bed never slept in. Kataryna tore through the palace searching for her, then on to the docks when she concluded she was not in the palace. Upon arriving at the docks, she found them empty. All boats had left earlier that morning, leaving a devastated princess behind.

Prince Nicholas had just come of age to coronate as King of Salara. The only thing stopping it was he had to be married first. On their wedding night, a prince became king, a princess a queen and three kingdoms became one. With the union of Kataryna and Nicholas, Pavlone, Salara and Holan were to be ruled as one.

†

With each full moon that rose, the new queen found her heart became a little colder and smaller. Until one full moon when her heart was no more and the Prophecy was at hand.

†

Several moons after being wed, Renaldo reminded Kataryna an heir was needed. Then another plan formed in Renaldo's head. Renaldo decided to use her future children as a reason for the queen to conquer and consume the lands surrounding them. He would fill her head with the delusion that she needed to conquer those around her to keep her children safe.

Kataryna demanded that Nicholas spend twice a day in her bed trying to make an heir. Within a fortnight Thalia informed Kataryna she was with child. She was stunned it had happened so quickly.

That morning, when the threads of the prophecy were starting to unravel, was one of those points in time when Kataryna thought about the path her life had taken over the past seasons. She lay in bed massaging her protruding stomach, feeling another spasm ripple through her. So much had changed. She now lived in Salara with her king, a king who was not a king at all.

Kataryna found him to be useless in ruling. Nicholas spent his days and nights in his study with his parchments. He fancied himself a bard and wanted nothing more than to be left alone with his stories. He had a bed moved into the study, so he would never have to leave his works. On occasion, she would find articles of clothing strewn on the floor and one of the palace guards lying beside him. She would then turn and leave before either man woke.

Kataryna found his ruling reprehensible. She did not care who warmed his bed at night as long as he left her alone.

57

He was pathetic as a man as well. She came to rule in his place instead.

†

Renaldo stayed by Kataryna's side, changing his plans as he saw greatness emerging in Kataryna and watched her become more ruthless as each full moon passed. This would work out better than his original plan. Renaldo guided her into wanting to conquer and seize everything that did not already belong to her kingdoms. Renaldo created a weapon. He kept King Theos from knowing what Kataryna was becoming. He sent reports back to Pavlone that everything was going beautifully and that he would stay on for the next season to make sure she was well.

The birth of the twin heirs had been celebrated with abandon. Kataryna spoke to no one of the dream of her mother telling her she would have a son and a daughter. She had been told to name the son Aiden and the girl Bryanne. Aiden would be known as Fiery and Bryanne as Strong One.

King Theos had hoped Aiden and Bryanne would bring about Kat's mothering instinct, causing her to step aside. Instead, the births had the opposite effect; it made her want more power. She wanted to give her children the world.

†

Over the two long years that passed since the wedding, Kataryna could not help but think back from time to time on what might have been. If only Raven had waited, she would have gone with her. She would have left her privileged life behind to be with the only person that would

58

ever hold her heart. Kataryna often returned to that morning and mulled it over in her mind. When she had left Raven in the hall, Kataryna had been happy, happier than she had ever known in her life. She then found her world turned upside down.

That seemed so long ago to her. She now had two-year-old twins and was with child again.

Yet she was content. Now no man would need to touch her again. With the birth of this, her third child, she would have more than two heirs, in case anything was to happen to one of them.

Kataryna had found long ago that she preferred the company of the female guards, which she had started to train in earnest to replace the male palace guards that she promoted to serve in her ever growing army. Never before had women been permitted to hold such high positions, but she still kept Pelor by her side. Kataryna trusted no one else in the coveted position of her personal guard. He would die for her and for her children.

Even as her heart hardened she couldn't deny Renaldo the time away to visit with Theos. The only time Renaldo left her side was to travel to Pavlone to comfort King Theos when he became lonely in the palace by himself. She even felt a moment of regret when Renaldo informed her that King Theos felt himself to be a king without a kingdom, after a messenger and guards from Salara arrived several moons before to inform him that all three kingdoms were to be ruled from Salara.

Another spasm moved through her belly. So much had changed since that first season. The princess, now the queen, ruled instead of the King. Even when Kataryna was with child the first time, she ruled as she had starting the very first day. The queen handed out swift justice. One such case came before her the previous morning. A young man, only twelve seasons old, was caught poaching on palace lands. Queen Kataryna found him guilty and condemned him to work in the mines until death, showing no mercy to anyone.

†

It was almost time for the baby's arrival. She had known it was to be a girl from the beginning. There was something different this time though. That sunrise before being awakened by the first spasms Kat dreamt her deceased mother was with her, telling Kataryna she would have a daughter and to name her Amara. Amara was to be known as The Eternal. She would be a seer. Kataryna's mother told her Amara *would know…the prophecy was at hand.*

Kataryna thought on what a seer could bring to her world. Amara would be her lifeline. She would help Kat to conquer. Amara would be her eyes whereas Aiden and Bryanne would be her strength. She decided to heed the dream just as she had the first one before the twins were to be born.

Through all the time she was with child, Kat continued her daily routine, including field training, just as she had the first time. She wanted to be the best. That very sunrise when she did not show for their morning session, Pelor went in search of her.

When Kataryna informed him it was time, Pelor brought Thalia to the queen's chambers. Thalia sat in a chair by the bed, mixing the herbs that would lessen the pain. Next he went to inform King Theos, who had arrived several hours earlier, that it was time.

Kat's spasms were coming closer together now, one upon the other.

Word spread that the next heir was about to be born. The farmers scrambled to find tributes, afraid of what the new ruler would do if they did not. Word had already been sent to the nobles, who assembled for the glorious event. Each brought with them items to present to the child that were worthy of gods. It had been over two seasons since the princess had become queen and the rumors of her brutality had since spread like fire. Many admitted to only their most trusted loyal friends that their queen was losing all compassion for her people.

Upon arrival at the palace in Salara, the nobles found the townspeople terrified. Each of the nobles thanked their god in their own way that they had brought the best they had to offer. Once in the palace they were brought into the banquet hall, which had been filled with food and drink. When they arrived, Renaldo informed them the birth of the prince or princess was near.

Kataryna told Pelor of her dreams. He was the only one she trusted with such knowledge. She did not completely trust Renaldo even though he had been with her through everything. There was something about his behavior that disturbed her. Something she could not put into words. When her mother came to her in the second dream Kataryna asked her if she could trust any other person than Pelor with her life or that of her children's. She watched in her dream as a single tear ran down her mother's face and then the dream abruptly ended.

Thalia had been timing the spasms and knew the child was ready to be born. "Kataryna, it is time. You must start to push." Thalia was one of only a handful that she permitted to call her by her first name. All others were to call her Queen or Your Majesty and several now began to call her Dragon, which she found she was becoming quite fond of.

Kataryna was panting hard as the pain had become excruciating. "By the Gods, Thalia, the pain was not this bad the first time. What is wrong? I know something is wrong... BY THE GODS...," she screamed as another pain ripped through her. The spasms turned from minor twinges to unbearable within a heartbeat and she was afraid.

†

Thalia could see the fear in Kataryna's face. She had not seen fear grace her features in many seasons. Thalia was worried. She knew this child was larger than the other two and might cause a problem during birthing. Moving to the foot of the bed she lifted the queen's bedcovers.

"Push child, you have to push now." She looked to see if the child's head was showing. It should have been by now. When she did not see it, she pushed the covers completely away, leaving only Kataryna's chest covered in her nightclothes. She pushed her legs as far apart as they would go, putting her tiny hand inside to feel for the head. She wanted to make sure the child had not turned around.

Upon finding the head right inside the opening, "One more push little one, just one more push."

"Thalia...get this baby out of me NOW! Oh, Gods does it hurt...and I AM pushing." Pushing with all she had left, Kataryna let out a scream that echoed through the chambers and down the hall. All that were waiting in her sitting chamber jumped from their places and started for the door. Pelor blocked their path telling them to relax.

"The head is coming out. You have to push, Kataryna." Then she saw it, the child's head was stuck in the opening. The child had come too fast and her opening had not fully expanded. "Kataryna, stop pushing...STOP. You have to control it and stop."

The queen raised her head from the bed. "What is wrong? I can feel it, something is not right. The pain is too much, by the Gods, Thalia, make the pain stop. Please, I am begging! Make it stop." She screamed again. "Please Thalia, make it stop...PLEASE!" Kataryna could not stop the scream that was wretched from her soul as she felt pain she had only felt once before; when her heart turned black as night.

Pelor heard Thalia call for him. That could mean only one thing. Something was wrong. He opened the door to the hallway, called one of the guards in and told her not to let anyone through to the inner room after he entered. In closing the door behind him, he was not prepared for the sight before him.

Before him was the queen, spread out, screaming in pain. Thalia was applying a salve around her opening where he saw the baby's head. Thalia had already called him aside several mornings ago, warning him the child may be too big and she might have problems giving birth. Sairana, Thalia's helper, now approached Kataryna with a cup of liquid.

"Pelor, I am going to need your help. Kataryna, you must drink all of what Sairana has. Do you understand, all of it. Pelor, come here." She motioned for him to come to her side.

Kataryna drank from the cup, some of it spilling down her neck. Within several heartbeats, the pain was no more and she relaxed. Thalia then went to work with Pelor's help. "I need you to clean off your dagger with the red liquid in the small bowl. The salve I put on her has numbed the area, she will not feel a thing."

Pelor did as told, bringing the knife back to her. The queen's eyes glazed over and she was mumbling about Amara coming into the world. Thalia took the knife, instructing him on what to do. She made precision cuts to widen the opening. She then slid the baby out, cut the cord and handed the child to Sairana to clean.

Thalia cleaned her of the afterbirth, directing Pelor to bring her the tray from the writing table. In fear of just this, she had already set out a tray with all the items she would need to sew Kataryna.

†

That nightfall, Kataryna's father sat by her side, marveling at the new little one. Theos watched as King Nicholas had come and looked at the child, held her and then handed her back to Theos, returning to his books and parchments not to be seen since. This was just as it had been with the twins. He could not have cared less whether they were born or not.

King Theos held the small sleeping bundle in his arms. "She is so beautiful, Kat. May the Gods watch over her and keep her safe." He handed Amara back to Kat so she could feed the infant. Kataryna was still weak and in a great deal of pain from the birth but Theos wanted to speak with her. He twisted his hands together deep in thought. He was unsure how to broach the subject without her temper flaring.

"Kat, I wanted to talk to you alone." He straightened the blanket that covered her a little. "I just wanted to ask you...are you happy?" He saw a feral grin cover her features.

"Am I happy? Right now, at this moment, I would have to say...NO! I just gave birth and had to be cut open like a melon. Do I look like I am happy, Father? Do I?" Her voice louder with each question.

"Kat, my child, that is…that is not exactly what I was asking. I was asking if you are happy with life itself. I know we have talked about it before. Have your feelings changed for Nicholas? Do you love him?" He reached over, replacing the covers that she had pushed down in order to feed Amara.

"Please Father! Love him? That will never happen. Do you want to know why? I am not capable of love. Tell me, Father, how could I love him when I have no heart or soul? I live only for my children and to rule over MY lands. Yes, Father, MY lands, not yours. They stopped being yours the day I realized what power truly felt like. Right now, Father, I hold all that power. Does that scare you?" She felt her strength returning and her courage growing as she finally confronted her father.

"You are a has-been and a pathetic ruler, Father. You could never hold the power that I do. The mines are producing four times what they were before I became queen and our halls are overflowing with the best food in the land. All of this is because of me, Father, not you. As for Nicholas, he is even more pathetic than you. He is useless and serves no purpose other than providing children as heirs to my kingdoms. Now if you will excuse me I am rather tired and wish to rest." She waved her hand toward the door and closed her eyes.

†

Just like that he had been dismissed, as if he were a common servant. Theos went to find Renaldo and Pelor to discuss this matter. Something had to be done, Kataryna was out of control. He feared not for himself but for his grandchildren and the people of his lands. They would always be his lands, no matter what his daughter thought. He just prayed it was not too late to save his daughter, so he sought out the people whom he thought could help him the most.

Just as Theos feared his pleas were ignored; neither of them would say a negative word about her. He returned to Pavlone that night, his thoughts weighing heavily on his mind. He needed time to think, time to find a way back for his daughter.

Theos, a king who was no longer a king, knew his only child was lost to him when four cycles of the moon after the birth of Amara, Kat and her army marched toward Lenara in the northern region.

†

It had come to the queen's attention that Lord Teran, who ruled Lenara, had been trying to gain support against her, trying to restore Theos as king. With Pelor at her side, she crushed Lord Teran's plans. This time she did not condemn the accused to the mines. She had something more drastic in mind for him.

Queen Kataryna had the lord beaten, then the still very much alive Teran brought before her in what had previously been his study. He knelt before her, pleading for his life and the life of his family, not knowing his wife and two sons were already dead. Only his daughter remained. She had just turned sixteen seasons and was betrothed to a son of a noble. She was not pretty, yet not homely. Kat kept her alive for a purpose, which she would disclose to him when the timing was perfect.

The queen sat in his beloved chair, the chair he sat in and plotted against her, while she listened to him blubber on and on. Finally being able to tolerate no more she stood, towering over him. "Shut up, you pathetic excuse for a man. How dare you! How dare you plot to overthrow me and now beg for my forgiveness. I am not in the mood."

She pulled her sword from its scabbard. Tossing it from one hand to the other; she wanted to toy with him before personally handing out her own form of justice for his treachery. "So, Teran, what do you think I should do with you? Hmm..." She ran the tip of the sword along his throat.

Teran begged once more for the lives of his family. "I don't care what you do with me but please let my family go. They had nothing to do with this. Please! I will do anything you want...anything."

Kataryna's laughter did not cease. She had to sit to stop from falling over, laughing so hard tears ran from her eyes. Finally regaining control, she wiped them from her face with the back of her hand. Kataryna threw her booted leg over the arm of the chair, giving off the air that she was ruler of the house which, of course, she was. The puny man had been brought to his knees. Now he would pay, first mentally, then with his life.

Angered by her laughter, Teran lifted his head and snarled, "You Bitch, how dare you!"

Silence filled the air.

"How dare I? No, you nasty little man, it is how dare you! I allowed you to rule this land even after I became Queen, knowing you had no tolerance for a woman ruling the lands. Well, you rule no more. This land and its people are now mine. Just as your wife was last night before she took her own life with the poison she kept in her dressing table. I must say she did an ample job begging for your life and the lives of her children while she attempted to pleasure me." The queen stood and squatted before him, a sneer replacing the smile on her face as she remembered the good Lady Elzbith in her bed the previous evening.

"Alas, your poor Elzbith wasn't up to the job. However did you stand her? She was the most pathetic creature that has ever graced my bed." Walking back to the table, she had her back to him. She knew he would not lunge toward her yet, for she had not pushed him quite far enough. Hearing him sob only sent her in for the kill. A man who sobbed was weak and served her no purpose.

"Your poor wife was incapable of doing what your daughter was born to do. By the Gods was she good. I have yet to sleep. Your daughter was so good, she kept pleasing me all night. I left her to recover in MY bedchambers to come deal with you." She once again sat in his chair, her leg thrown over the arm. She put her hand on her pubic area and rubbed.

"Mmm…yes, she was very good. She fucked me to within an inch of my life. Of course, I returned the favor of pleasure, only to find she was a virgin. Oh my, what was I to do?" An evil laugh escaped, the feral look once again replaced the look of innocence on her face.

She threw her booted foot on the floor with a thud, making sure he was paying attention. "What I did was fuck her till she screamed for no more. I told her the only way I would stop was if she pleasured me more. Funny thing about that, she happily agreed. What do you think of that, little man?"

He looked up at her and she saw the anger. This was what she wanted to see. She wanted him to fight back. "That's it, little man, fight back…I gave your wife and daughter such pleasure…pleasure like no man ever could."

Teran lunged for her and her blade moved swifter than the eye. The guards that had brought him in watched as his head rolled to the floor and landed with a sickening thud.

"Mount it on a pike then put it in the square for all to see. Let it serve as an example to those who would defy me. Spread word through the village that I am 'requesting' the presence of all in the square at first light. At present, I am going to retire for the evening. Find Rokyn; tell her I wish to see her."

Kataryna's appetite in the bedroom grew with each passing moon since becoming Queen. Some nightfalls she only wished for one of her favorites sharing her bed, while on other nights two or three. Rokyn, the head of the guards, was her favorite. Even then there was something missing. Yes there was passion and extreme pleasure but always there was a missing element that Kataryna just couldn't find in any of the women.

After killing the lord, she felt the effects upon herself. It was the same as battle lust and it needed to be appeased. She sat in the outer chamber of the room she claimed for herself, downing the last of the spirits. They flowed through her, warming her from within. Spirits and sex were the only things that kept the ice inside her at bay and completely consuming her. "Yeah sex. Gods know you cannot call it lovemaking…I would need to feel love to call it that. Or at the very least capable of feeling…something."

She listened as the outer door opened then closed and heavy booted footfalls approached. "You requested my presence, My Dragon. You have need of me?"

Kataryna looked up from her goblet. "Yes, I have need, lots of needs. However, the need I have now is you and the creature who lay in my bed, naked, filling me." With that, she stood and started for the inner chamber door discarding clothing as she went.

Through the darkness into the sunlight screams of pleasure rang through the outer chamber and the halls. The guard standing sentry through the night in the hall could only smile, knowing firsthand the gifts bestowed behind the heavy oak doors.

Near dawn, Kataryna had asked Rokyn to join her in bathing, knowing they had not been fully sated as of yet. Upon entering the bathing chamber, Kataryna quickly washed herself and then her bath mate. Suddenly, she felt herself pulled to her knees and turned facing away from Rokyn just as she felt both orifices entered. She cried out in pleasure and pain at the same time, being that the areas were so sensitive from the previous night's use. As the sun dawned and the townspeople made their way to the square Kataryna was extracting her now well-sated body from the tepid bathwater.

Sometime later while dressing, the queen came to a decision on what to do with Teran's daughter. She could not take her with her. Afraid the girl would attempt to avenge her family she called Rokyn into the study off the outer room and informed her of what she wanted done.

"I cannot take a chance that she will not try to avenge her family. Please see that she is taken to the nuns in the Outlands immediately. I will then meet you at the stables to go to the square."

As they entered the town square on their horses they found the townspeople and farmers alike all gathered, cowering in fear. Before them was the head of their lord on a pike for all to see. They feared what had befallen him would be the same for them. The queen brought her horse to a stop beside the ghastly head and observed the crowd.

The being sitting atop the powerful black horse was not the princess or even the queen they had known. Gone were the beautiful dresses and the obvious femininity. In their place were harshness, brutality, black leather breeches, a sword, and a tunic the color of freshly spilled blood.

"Listen to me, all of you. This man was a fool. A fool who thought he could dethrone me. I will be brought down by no man, woman, or child. Be it known—the Lord and his family are no more. Are there any among you who feel as he did?" She scanned the crowds and found none that would meet her eyes.

"Good! It will save me time. Spread the word that I will no longer tolerate further uprisings. Anyone who is found to be conspiring against me will meet the same fate, or worse. He died quickly. Those that follow will not be so lucky. Now go home and reflect on this day and what you have learned here."

The queen rode from the square, Pelor on one side, Rokyn on the other and Renaldo behind her. "We need to go to Pavlone. There is something there I need to take care of. Send a scout ahead to inform them of our arrival."

Silence engulfed them all, each lost in their own thoughts. All noticed a change in her that morning. She was angrier and more volatile than they had ever seen before. The silence lasted the entire four nightfalls that it took to make their way to Pavlone.

✝

Kataryna found her father, a few guards still loyal to him, and the last remaining lords in what had once served as his war room.

The doors burst open and the queen strode in followed by her guards and Renaldo. All that could be heard in the silence were her heavy leather riding boots, clomping on the tile floor and the metal clanging of her swords at her waist.

Theos's anger burst forth. "How dare you come in here unannounced!"

"I dare because I am the ruler! I dare because I am the queen! I dare because I accuse you of treason against your queen!" She threw her worn leather gloves on the table as she approached him. She went in for the kill.

"I dare because Teran's daughter informed me of an interesting little item. You, my dear father, had just visited her father for the third time in as many moons. Why were you there? Hmm…let me guess. Could it be to plot against me?" King Theos sat unmoving as she looked down upon him.

"Please, Father, tell me she was lying. Tell me she lied to me as she had her mouth on me pleasuring me through the night." It happened faster than she expected. With the reflexes of lightning, he stood and slapped her hard across the face.

"You are not my daughter. I do not know who you have become. I already knew what you had done before the arrival of your scout. You have become a murderer and a whore. Do you think your mother would be proud of you?" He stood before her defiant.

"Listen to me, old man. How dare you speak of my mother! She was a saint to put up with the likes of you. As far as what I am…I am what I was born to be—a ruler. The only reason you are not dead is because you are my father, and for no other reason."

She surveyed the room. Within the room stood all the people necessary to observe and carry out her orders. "Because you are my father I will not ask for your head, which is the punishment for being found guilty of treason, even though I have every right to. I will instead banish you from my lands for the rest of your life." She turned to Pelor. "Get him out of here. I have business to take care of."

Theos's eyes beseeched Renaldo, begging for his help as he was led past him. "I will watch over her and try," Renaldo softly told his spouse, even though he knew he would not.

Renaldo, as always, would encourage Kataryna to conquer, to spill blood, and become the most ruthless ruler ever known.

✝

Five seasons passed since the birth of Aiden and Bryanne, which made it four since the birth of Amara and three since the banishment of Theos. Kataryna sat at the table in her bedchamber as Delfina applied the last of the dye to her hair. She had become bored with everything in her life. Her children were the only things that kept her going.

The queen decided that change was in order, starting with her appearance. She asked Thalia to give Delfina the ingredients she would need to complete the permanent dye to change the color of her hair. Her beautiful long hair was gone. When Thalia walked into the inner chamber, she had been in the process of cutting it off herself. Kataryna heard her gasp and then Delfina followed behind her, almost dropping the bowl she was carrying.

Delfina stepped around Thalia, who could only stand and stare. She cautiously approached her. "Oh little one, what have you done?"

The queen turned to look at her. "I am tired of my long hair, I'm tired of the color, and today starts a new day! Now get on with it."

Thalia deposited the items on the table and backed out of the room slowly. Delfina stepped behind Kat, picked up the hair trimmers. "Let me see if I can do something with this mess. If you wanted it cut, child, you could have just asked me. You did not need to make this disaster." She proceeded to make some semblance of the mess Kat had created.

Kataryna let Delfina's scolding wash over her. Delfina had been as a mother should have been to her. It warmed her, just a little, to know that someone still cared for her. She and Thalia were the only two that Kataryna would let get away with such behavior and even with that, she would not let them say too much before putting a stop to it.

"Delfina...I told you..." She tried to turn her head to look at her but Delfina moved it back around.

"Hold still or I'll take your ear off. Now let me fix this." A few moments later, she lay the instrument on the table, picking up the dye.

Sometime later, once the dye had set, Delfina washed the remnants from her hair. "What do you think?"

Holding the mirror, the queen looked upon the face of someone new. What looked back at her was not Kataryna, nor the queen but what had become of them. Gone were the long black tresses, replaced by bronzed short spikes. No hair came lower than her ear. It was the Dragon whose reflection she saw.

The sight made Delfina even more fearful for Kat's soul. "Oh little one, I fear for you. I fear for what is happening to your heart, to your soul. You have seemed so unhappy these past seasons. I fear you will be lost to us forever."

A growl erupted from Kataryna's chest and she did nothing to stop it. "Do not dare to question me, Delfina! I am who I was born to be. This is my fate. I am the Dragon." Evil laughter replaced the growl. "You know not of what you speak! You speak of my heart and my soul. Those have long since shriveled and died. They left me long ago." She threw the mirror onto the table and stood.

"I must dress and take care of some business. Please inform Rokyn to have King Nicholas brought to the war room immediately!" New moon by new moon over the past season Renaldo slowly turned her mind against Nicholas. She had always thought of him as useless and never paid him any mind. Renaldo slowly convinced her that the only use he served was to possibly plot against her. Before she could let that happen, something needed to be done. She admitted that she had grown tired of his presence. He was useless, taking up space and serving no purpose to her whatsoever. It was not as if she needed him to provide her with heirs any longer.

She stepped to the bed and started dressing in what had become her new attire of late—black leather breeches, a blood-red tunic, wide black leather belt, coupled with an ankle-length black leather sleeveless overcoat. The last items added were her swords. The short sword was sheathed in a holster upon her leg. She put the jewel-crusted scabbard through its loop on her belt. Finally, she picked up her sword.

Kataryna looked over the sword that had been specially made for her over a season ago. This one fit her grip perfectly. The hilt of it was shaped like a dragon with blue diamonds set as the eyes. She held it in her left hand and looked upon the dragon, then upon her own hand that held it.

Had that hand truly taken lives? Was this hand the same hand that once touched something beautiful, as beautiful as the memory that was now fading into obscurity? She could scarcely remember what the woman had looked like, what she had felt like. Kat looked upon her hand once more, then at the hilt. An idea formed and she called for the one standing guard.

†

Having changed her plan, it was sunset when she strode into the war room where a crowd gathered. Upon seeing the change of appearance, all in the room stopped talking. They looked from her newly altered hair to the fresh dragon tattoo on her left arm. The tattoo started on the back of her hand and went up the entire length of her arm.

Already assembled were Pelor, seated next to her chair at the end of the table. On the other side of her was Renaldo. Seated along the length were others from her military and several lords whom she knew would not betray her, therefore she had left them in power.

Standing guard at the opposite end of the table was Rokyn. Beside her sat the king in what was not his usual chair. The ruling king always occupied the other end of the table. That was until Queen Kataryna came into power. He found himself treated as a common lord and was seated at the opposite end. No queen in history had ever occupied a seat at the war table. The seating did not go unnoticed by a single soul who entered the room.

76

The servants finished setting the food on the table and left as quickly as they could. Silence replaced idle chatter as they ate. All felt the tension. They knew this was someone's last meal, especially since meals were never served in the room prior to this day.

Replacing the empty dishes were pitchers of dark ales with fresh goblets. Shocking all, the queen went from person to person, filling each of their cups from the pitchers. She handed Rokyn hers upon filling it, then turned to the king to fill his last.

Lifting her own jewel-encrusted goblet in the air all became deathly quiet. "What now seems like many seasons ago I became queen as well as ruler of this land and all those who fell under its protection, which I know came as a shock to many of you. Would you rather have been ruled by a spineless, gutless little boy who would have become king?" She looked around the room and saw stunned expressions.

"Knowing he was to replace King Theos, I made a decision that day about what was best for this country and my people. Again today, I do what is best for this country and now for my children." She quietly withdrew the dagger hidden within her coat.

"Tell me any of you, when is a king not a king?" Hearing no one answer, she continued. "It is when he commits treason. Nicholas here has told false allegations against the queen, the ruler of your lands. Does any person here stand by him?" The queen looked from person to person, not one stood up for him.

"Then judgment is delivered."

King Nicholas made as if to stand, but was held in place by a powerful hand. Looking up it was Rokyn's hand on his shoulder. "What am I to have done? I have done nothing. I have left you alone as you requested."

Kataryna's head bent back in laughter. "What have you done? My, how we forget, do we not? Did you not just last moon make a statement to my father, Renaldo, that you had severe misgivings about how I was ruling and felt I should step down and let you rule? Do you deny these words?"

†

Knowing he was beaten, he regretted saying those words to Renaldo, whom he thought he could trust. Yes, he knew several of Renaldo's dirty secrets. All had thought he never paid attention to anything but his scrolls. They, however, would have been surprised to learn that he was actually listening to those plotting and scheming around him. Nicholas gathered the information to use if such a day as this was to ever come to pass. He once more attempted to stand. "I deny nothing. I…" He felt the dagger plunge into his chest.

Nicholas looked down and watched as Kataryna pulled it from his chest and threw it onto the table. Sinking into the chair, his life oozed from his chest. He vowed he was not taking all the blame alone. He begged her to listen, that he had something more important than his own life to tell her. As he took his last breaths he told her of Renaldo's greatest secret. He told of her mother's fate. He related the tale of how Renaldo killed her after giving birth to Kataryna. With his last breath Nicholas told her the only thing that mattered to Renaldo was the power and the wealth.

†

As Nicholas told his story, the fury grew within her. How could she have been so gullible? How could she have believed Renaldo? Any shred of humanity left in her vanished as the reality of treachery sank into her very core. She looked down the length of the table to gaze upon Renaldo's face as Nicholas told his tale. No emotion showed as she listened to the tale.

Kat looked at Renaldo once more. This time a feral look overtook her features.

Renaldo knew something was wrong. What is he telling her? I must stop him.

Kat saw Renaldo as he moved to stand and open his mouth to speak. She waved a guard toward him and bellowed. "Silence and sit."

Renaldo had no choice as he was forced back into the chair.

Upon seeing the fear in Renaldo's eyes, she knew it to be true. Her whole life had been a lie. Thoughts flew through her mind like a runaway mule cart. Would things have turned out differently if he had not killed her? Would she be a caring, loving wife instead of the heartless, soulless bitch that she had become or was this her destiny all along, even if mother had lived?

She shook the thoughts from her head as they no longer had a place in her life. Without contemplating her actions, she picked up the dagger she had withdrawn from King Nicholas's chest and launched it down the table with lightning speed.

The dagger flew so fast Renaldo only had time to draw one last breath. When the weapon hit its mark, imbedding itself in Renaldo's forehead, Pelor and the lord on the other side of him jumped from their chairs. Startling everyone further, she jumped up on the table and walked its length to the middle.

"Quiet!" It came out not as a scream, but a bellow for all to notice.

"Let it be known through the lands that today a traitorous king and a traitorous stepfather were brought to justice. Alas, also let it be known that on this day something very sad has taken place. Tell them Queen Kataryna died as well. In her place now rules the Dragon. Never again is the queen's name to be spoken. If anyone dare question what has happened to their queen, they will be condemned to death. Go...go back to your posts and your lands! Rokyn, get someone to clean up this mess." She jumped from the table. The thud from her boots echoed through the room.

Hand on the hilt of her sword she made her way across the room. Her body a tightly wound coil, she was ready for anything; she half expected at least one of them to confront her. When her eyes met Pelor's she saw a brief moment of grief before it was gone. She knew he, of all, would not stand against her. He would always be there, just as he had since they were children running around the palace grounds causing all kinds of trouble. She stopped in front of him and waited. She waited for the condemnation to spew forth from him. None came.

Instead, he grasped her right forearm and bowed his head. "My Dragon, it will be an honor to serve you as I served those before you. I pledge my life and my loyalty to you."

"Thank you, Pelor, I would have expected no less from you." At that, she walked out the door into the hallway and a new existence.

Word spread through the lands by the rise of the next sun. All mourned the loss of their queen and feared for their lives as they heard the rapidly spreading tales of what the Dragon had done in the war room. Tales were told of how she executed the king then Renaldo and lastly their queen. They did not mourn their queen; their sorrow was for the little girl they had known whose heart had turned black and soul had withered.

Chapter Four

The next ten seasons brought with them tremendous change, not just throughout the lands but within the palace as well. The Dragon became the most feared creature to have ever lived. Rumors spread she was not even human, that she was instead a creation of an evil witch from the western region. The main ruling palace once more became Pavlone, because it was centrally located.

Taxes were imposed that were beyond what any were capable of paying. Any ships that docked in Pavlone were expected to pay heavy tariffs imposed by the Dragon. If unable to pay those tariffs, goods were confiscated and sometimes the ships themselves were taken.

In many instances if there was a beautiful woman on board, she was taken and given to the Dragon as part of the payment, in addition to the money. In several others cases, the women, if beautiful enough, were received in lieu of money.

The Dragon and her armies, led by herself and Rokyn, swept through the lands consuming everything. They conquered every new region with great ease. With every new season, the regions fell easier and her armies grew. While their numbers grew, not a single person dared to challenge her or her authority.

Upon taking over a town, village or city, she would make sure her armies did not loot, pillage, or rape. Only when the villagers put up a fight, did she allow her armies to act out, she wanted to maintain a shred of respect for the position of authority. She, however, never denied herself the occasional young bedmate from the villages, if the mood struck her.

To her, if the people...her people, thought she might spare them the brutality that such treatment would bring, they would follow her to the ends of the earth. They also knew if they disobeyed her, they would be dealt with accordingly.

Any who had gone against her were put to death, their heads put on pikes in the town squares for all to see, just as she had from the beginning. As the legend of the Dragon spread over the seasons, many children turned into warriors in her armies. They found themselves lured by the power the Dragon held. Some were forced into service when she caught sight of them as she rode through the streets.

†

Her own children grew to rule beside her. Tragedy struck in one of the northern regions when the Fates dealt the Dragon a heavy blow. Rokyn, always the first into battle, was killed during one of the worst they had fought. It had always been a possibility but it hurt nonetheless. She made herself not care, not feel the pain. She mourned her loss and by nightfall told all that her daughter, Bryanne, was now in training to be captain of the guards.

Two seasons had passed since that battle. Bryanne, at fourteen seasons, full Captain of the Guards, stood beside the Dragon as she made her son Aiden in charge of the archers and scouts. Her youngest, Amara, looked on, knowing in her soul what was to come. It first came to her in dreams, then in flashes while awake. She tried not to dwell on them, instead working harder on her studies to become a healer.

Amara was very different from her siblings. They were loud, where she was quiet and reserved. They became servants of the Dragon, doing her bidding, where she followed her heart, awaiting HER return. Where the others had their mother's black eyes, Amara's were very different. Her eyes were not her mother's nor her father's, nor any others ever in the royal line. When one looked into her eyes what looked back at them was clear as crystal, with just the tiniest hint of blue.

Each time the Dragon looked into them over the seasons, they reminded her of someone; someone long since dead but she could not remember whom. After a while, she stopped trying and never looked her daughter in the eyes again. Because to look into them had, for some unknown reason, become too painful even for her, the Dragon.

†

The Dragon's youngest, many seasons before at the age of five, had foretold of the coming.

The coming of the *one*...

The *one* that would bring about the downfall of the Dragon.

It came to her one nightfall in a dream. It was an image of a woman with long, flowing hair with a tattoo upon her face. It was a design of blue and green upon a face that carried down upon the neck onto the shoulder. This woman would bring hope; a future for Pavlone. Furthermore, she would bring a future for the queen who was no more.

The queen would be restored to what she once was.

†

As all destinies were coming into their own within the palace walls, another's was coming full circle on the seas.

Alane Hotchkin

Chapter Five

What would you do for love?
Would you kill for love?
Would you plunder for love?
Would you ultimately die for love?

What would you do when your soulmate tried to destroy your love? Would you fight for it, would you walk away? Or would you gain strength and return to fight another day?

Would you lose your true self?

The ultimate question being: could you convince the owner of your heart and soul that you were destined to be together?

Betrayal by your soulmate can be the cause of all that happens to you. It can define your destiny; it can change it from its original course.

You give everything you are willingly to make you complete. You have no choice in the matter. Before you know what has happened you are empty, you are soulless, and you become something you are not; someone *she* would loathe.

86

✝

When Raven set sail that morning some fifteen seasons before, she felt dead inside. She had given her heart and soul willingly to Kataryna. As she repacked her meager belongings that night, betrayal washed over her making her numb. Disbelief and anger set in when she reached the docks. By the time the ship set sail she was hollow.

Over the seasons that followed, she let the blackness fill the void where her heart and soul should have been. When she left so long ago, she was nothing more than a petty thief, even though she had taken a life. The first life she had taken had been in self-defense, since then...

✝

Arriving at the docks that fateful morning, Raven checked out all of the ships docked in the harbor. She informed Renaldo she did not want to be on any ship that was carrying families. He searched for a ship that looked a little less than reputable. Raven came upon a merchant ship being loaded by heavily armed, scruffy-looking men. She informed Renaldo that ship would do fine. She was very curious why a merchant ship would need such men, however, she did not care. She asked to see the captain of the ship and was greeted with laughter in return.

Raven pulled the closest man off the plank leading to the ship and held him up close and personal to her. When his face was within an inch of hers, he could see the emptiness in her eyes. "I said I want to speak with the captain...now!" Then she threw him into the water.

When the disgusting, rotund little man that called himself Captain stepped forth and saw who wanted passage on his ship, his mind filled with lecherous thoughts. His actions proved to be his downfall when two nightfalls later he invited her to dine with him.

Captain Rouschan sent a crimson dress made of the finest silk for her to wear. She laughed when the deliverer turned and left. Did he truly expect her to wear such a thing? She instead pulled on her black leather trousers, her black tunic, and boots. She then gathered her long hair back, braided it, tied it off with a piece of leather; letting the braid fall down her back.

To say the captain was displeased was mild. He roared and bellowed at her to put the dress on. When she refused, he boasted he could beat her into putting it on. She proceeded to laugh, knowing she could take him before he took his next breath.

Her laughter setting him on edge, he decided against pushing her to wear it. He liked the arrogance in her attitude but saw something in her eyes, though, that made him wary—blackness, a deep well of nothingness.

During the meal, the captain spoke of much wealth to be made with the right crew. Raven knew of what he spoke, and the fact that he was willingly laying out all his plans to her told her he did not plan on her being around very long. He wanted to make his merchant ship a little more profitable. There was only one way to do so, turn it into a pirate ship. She felt in her gut that he would not last one single sunrise as a pirate.

On the table before Raven sat a banquet fit for a king. Not one meal since she came on board had been what she would have called fit for humans to eat. Yet here the captain sat with a bounty. She ate her fill quickly, yet she did not gorge herself, needing to be light on her feet.

A plan formed in her mind. It wasn't a small one or a nice one, but a hideous one. She would make it as a pirate and she had found her ship. Her heart became as black as any pirate's heart that still beat and colder than any that already met their fate.

✝

The War God became pleased with what he had created and Hades awaited her arrival at his gates, for he knew she was not to die at sea but on land. To obtain her soul he would willingly conspire with the War God to cheat the sea out of his greatest creation.

✝

Raven knew the captain would be stupid enough to try something, it was just a matter of when. She finished her rum, setting the cup on the table. He had made sure throughout the meal her cup was never empty. She knew he was trying to get her drunk, so that she would not be able to outmaneuver him.

Wiping her hands on her breeches, she continued watching him. Raven knew right where his eyes were lingering.

Licking his lips, he pushed his plate aside.

She had endured worse in her young life. However, this man would soon find out who was the stronger of the two.

89

Since he provided her with such a fine meal, he felt it was her obligation to repay his kindness. He stood, retrieving his pipe from the table behind them. "Fine meal, was it not? Better than what you have eaten on board yet?"

Raven nodded. "Aye, it was." She watched out the corner of her right eye, as he got closer.

"And how will you repay me for my generosity? Do you perchance have money?" He set the pipe on the table.

Moving rapidly he pulled her from her chair, roughly clenching her left breast with his fat, small hand. Shaking off the pain, she let him squeeze it, then pull hard on her nipple. "You like that, don't you? You're a whore, just like all the rest of them."

He rubbed his body against hers, his hard manhood already pushing his pants out. As he rubbed it against her, it grew larger and larger. "Yeah, I like it, little man, but only one little problem." She turned him and pushed him against the table, her chair now to the left of her. "You're a man."

Luckily for Raven, she could handle a sword equally well with both hands. She pushed the dishes to the floor and him onto the table. Bringing his hips up from the table, he pushed against her. He had no idea she was reaching for her sword that was hanging on her chair. Drawing it from its case Raven quickly stepped back, putting distance between the two of them.

Seeing the sword pointing at him, he flew into rage. "You bitch! How dare you! I took you in. I fed you."

Raven shook her head. "But you will never, ever, touch me, little man. I want this ship and this crew. I have plans and they do not include you."

Captain Rouschan made a fatal mistake when he tried to have his way with her after their meal. He found himself with a sword in his round belly. He then slipped from the sword to the floor. After cleaning her sword on his trousers leg Raven returned it to its scabbard. She then threw his lifeless body onto the deck of the ship. All movement ceased and she felt the crew's eyes land upon her.

"Listen and listen well, for I will not repeat myself. This little, greasy man was no more than a boil on life. I, however, am a lot more. I am Captain of this ship now and any not willing to follow may get off now and try their hand at swimming. As for him, dump him overboard and feed the sharks." She watched as two men stepped forward and followed her orders.

"Who is first mate of this ship?" Scanning the men's faces, what she saw puzzled her. If not mistaken, she saw admiration. Out of the crowd of men stepped not a large man but neither was he tiny. He was just as slimy as the captain had been. He, however, was what kept the other men in line; he was their keeper. She studied him, then the others.

Raven knew something was off balance. She could not immediately put her finger upon it. She looked once more at the lifeless body as it was taken off the deck, then to the first mate and on to the men themselves. She saw fear. "Ah, now I see."

She acted so swiftly she surprised even herself. Drawing her sword, Raven turned and ran the first mate through. She then cleaned her sword, once more, on the trouser leg of the first mate and returned it to its home. "I do not believe in enslaving my crew. All should have a fair share, for do not all of you share equally in the risk? I will protect you as you protect me. This is what I believe in, do you?"

The crew looked to one another, then to their new captain. Raven knew what they saw. "Forget I am a woman. If it makes it easier, think of me as a man. Remember only what I can do. Now I ask you once more, will you follow me without question? Without thought?"

Since her arrival upon the ship, the crew had watched her closely. They considered it a bad omen to have a woman on board so they kept a watchful eye. What they saw surprised them; she was not a bit of fluff. She was one of them. She wore trousers as they did, joined in on the ribald stories and when the first mate had been bold and asked her which one of them she would prefer to bed, she told them none of them were pretty enough. The first mate eyed her with disgust while all others envied her the boldness and courage she showed.

Without hesitation one by one, the crew stepped forward with an "Aye, Capt'n…"

Raven looked each man in the eye then took a step back. "Who among you is the best swordsman? And who among you truly leads this ragtag bunch of misfits?" In order for them to be in as good of health as they seemed, she knew someone among the crew was looking out for all of them.

All the men stepped back except one. Gezana was the best at every weapon known, but not only that, he could also read and write. He was the man the entire crew was faithful to, what he said went untouched. He was the one who took their beatings for them. The only thing that had stopped him from defending himself before this was he knew Rouschan and his first mate would hurt the others for his insurrection.

"I am Gezana; it appears I have been selected. I will serve you well. What heading shall we set to?" He stood hands behind his back awaiting his orders.

She remembered the captain saying there was much wealth in the west. That also meant the trading ships would be laden with wealth. "Set a course west, Gezana. Please join me in my office once we are under way." Turning to leave, she hesitated. "Throw him over." She looked down at the dead man and knew this was only the first blood to be shed by their hands.

Raven found the cabin boy waiting outside what was now her office—the office of the captain of the ship. She looked down upon his blond head, waiting for him to look at her. "Young lad…"

"Lorenzo, Capt'n." He never looked up as she spoke. To do so had been beaten out of him.

"Lorenzo, look up at me." She waited yet still he did not. "Lorenzo, you need not fear me. I do not beat a person unless they deserve it, much less a young lad like you. Now look up at me."

The head slowly, fearfully tilted upward. "What may I do for you, Capt'n Raven?"

She chuckled. "Much better, young man. How old are you lad?"

"Not sure, Capt'n. I was six seasons old when I was taken and that was quite some time ago."

Raven knew then that he was older than he looked. He looked as if he had not eaten in many moons, for he was skin and bones. She opened the doors to the office and glanced about. "Interesting… What I want for you to do is clean this office up. Throw overboard all of the…" She picked up what looked to be some form of leftover food that was beyond petrified, "…trash."

She wiped her hand on her trousers. "Disgusting pig is what he was. Just please clean this place up. First, though, go to my cabin, clean it out of everything you know I will not want and thoroughly scrub it and burn the bed sheets. I do not care to catch any disease he might have had. Please, if you could find something to replace them at least temporarily until we make port and I may buy new ones. I will meet with Gezana then you can return here."

As an afterthought she added, "Oh, and please, Lorenzo, get some food in you. You look as if you would blow away in the first storm we pass through."

Lorenzo stood for a moment with a puzzled look upon his face. Then ever so slowly a shy smile crept upon his face. Lorenzo nodded acknowledgment and was on his way. Raven guessed he was so used to being beaten he did not know how to act. She would change that. She would show him he deserved respect. She may be an ice-cold bitch, but she would treat them with respect if they so deserved it. If they did not, may the Gods have mercy on their souls when she sent them to meet their God.

†

She looked around the cabin that would serve as her office. Size wise it was bigger than most of the rooms she had ever slept in. It, however, was filthy dirty with papers and garbage covering every available space. In the middle of the room sat an old well-used table with a chair on each of the two longer sides. Hanging securely from several hooks on the ceiling were oil lanterns. She acknowledged that at least he had the common sense to do that, otherwise he ran the risk of burning the ship to nothing. She turned each up to observe the room better.

Raven sorted through the papers and charts on the table, discarding what she did not want onto the floor with the rest of the rubble she had pushed from the tabletop. A short time later, she heard a knock on the door. "Enter."

Raven pointed to the chair across from her. Tipping her chair back on two legs, Raven threw her booted feet onto the table and locked her hands behind her head. She looked at the ceiling as if deep in thought, so Gezana sat quietly.

What seemed an eternity later, she smiled, lowering her eyes to meet his. "So tell me, would you follow me to Hades if I asked?" Crossing her arms in front of her, she waited for his answer.

Surprising Raven, he answered without hesitation. "Yes."

"Would this crew?"

Again without hesitation, "Yes."

"Then answer this as well. Is there any man upon this ship who should not be here for what I have in mind?"

"Without knowing what you have in mind, Capt'n, I cannot answer that." The new captain smiled a full smile, yet it never reached her eyes. It did not hold the pleasantness he had seen before and there was a gleam in her eyes, a very wicked one. It told him what she had in mind. "I see. Aye, Capt'n, there are several here that would not be good. Might I suggest leaving them in the next port? I know of one or two that will do to replace them."

Taking her feet from the table Raven set her chair down with a thud. Leaning forward she was inches from his face. "Would you stake your life on theirs?"

"Yes, without question. They are all good men and to be trusted." He thought a moment before continuing. "If I may ask, Capt'n, what will you do with Lorenzo? You would not have need of him as the previous captain had."

"He can stay. I have already given him several tasks. He can do the small duties above ship, as long as he keeps my cabin and this space clean. He is not to be beaten ever again or touched in any other manner. Make sure all are aware of this. Now go through the list of men and give me their strengths and weaknesses."

†

They went down the list man by man, item by item. When mealtime came Lorenzo brought food to them in the office, then sat outside the door waiting in case they might have need of him. Raven knew he had not gone far. When they were finished, she called for him. He was through the door like a shot. "Yes, Capt'n?"

"We are finished, please take away the dishes." She heard Gezana chuckle under his breath.

When the young man had shut the door behind him, she spoke up. "I know...I know...I think the poor thing is so grateful he would wash my feet for me. Please keep a watchful eye on him. So tell me how someone who can read and write has become a pirate."

"Aye, my Captain, I was once a captain in the Baul navy. I became a little disillusioned when I was ordered by my commander to sink a merchant ship carrying women and children that might have harbored a criminal aboard. At the next port I gathered my belongings, went ashore, and never looked back. I have since heard that commander lost his life to mutiny." Gezana smiled, knowing there was just a little justice left in the world. "I never let harm come to women or children. Why should they be punished for the deeds of men?"

Pirates were supposed to think differently, but he and Raven were not your usual pirates. Without thought, those exact words slipped from his lips.

Raven roared with laughter. "Yes, Gezana! We indeed are not your normal pirates. Now down to more business. How many military ships do you think we will encounter along this route?" She pointed to the map. They sat formulating plans and strategies and long after the moon had come out they finally finished and each retired to their own cabins.

Raven was speechless when she entered her new cabin. Lorenzo had not only scrubbed the cabin top to bottom, but according to the small note he left on her night table, he had replaced all the linens from Gezana's private stash and moved her few meager belongings into the room.

†

As planned, at the next port they traded out three of the crew, restocked the ship, and were on their way by nightfall. Not wanting to draw attention to themselves, they decided not to stay in port overnight. They never stole from any port they docked at; no one knew who they were. When docked they made sure the merchant vessel flag was flying and Raven never left the ship while in port. At sea, the ship remained looking like a merchant ship and still raised the merchant flag when approaching other ships with the same flag sailing in the wind. By the time their victim realized what was happening they were defenseless and Raven and her men had already boarded the unsuspecting ship.

Raven and her crew stripped ship after ship bare of all currencies. Furthermore, they took anything that could be sold or bartered. They would hit a number of ships then lay low for several moons in an inlet they had found on an island that no one knew existed. Their ship would just fit through the narrow passage into the bay when the tide was high.

None knew what to make of the stories that ran rampant throughout the shipping lanes. Rumors flew of a ship disappearing into thin air with a female captain. No living person had ever come upon such a creature.

As her reputation grew, Raven became known as El Diablo. Rumors spread that if your ship met up with El Diablo's, you would forfeit not only your ship, but your soul as well. Sailors told stories of El Diablo eating your soul if she caught you defenseless.

Most chose not to believe El Diablo was a woman, but a man; for a simple female could not be capable of the things that El Diablo had done. Raven grew to like the name she had been given.

Only once had someone tried to put an end to their looting. After their first couple of seasons plundering merchant ships, the Lord from Lenara sent some of his troops and his ships after them. In the end, the soldiers lost their lives and their ships. Since that time, no one had been tempted to stop them.

Gezana never said a word as he watched her become more and more ruthless as each season passed. Whenever possible Raven and her crew left few, if any, alive to tell the tales. Plenty of blood was shed and many lives were lost. Over the seasons, they sank ships without remorse, killing most of the crew aboard. One thing she did not condone was the taking of the lives of women and children. If they came across a ship that had families on them, they would only strip them bare, leaving enough for them to survive until rescued. Twice over the seasons, they came across a ship that was better than theirs. Raven would keep the better ship, sinking their old one. Switching ships helped as well in case anyone was tracking them by looking for their old ship.

The several men they lost during battle were replaced when Gezana found new ones he felt could be trusted. Over the seasons Raven and her crew amassed great wealth. Such amounts of wealth were unheard of. Most pirates spent as fast as they plundered but Raven, as well as Gezana, instilled the men with a little common sense along the way. As a result, only once or twice a season did the men splurge and lose all they had acquired in their latest raid.

Within the inlet upon the island, they built lodging for each of them. When one man was lost and a new man joined them, he would be given the dead man's lodging and half of his wealth. The remainder went into the kitty to obtain everyday staples they all used when they could not plunder what they needed.

When Raven's need for pleasure grew too much, the ship would stay in a port a few extra hours, Gezana would bring a woman to her that he knew would silence her needs, and they would be gone after sunset. He had tried to draw information about her past from her, but she refused to talk about anything before they met. She continued to keep her promise to her men by keeping them wealthy and safe.

Lorenzo continued to clean and cook for Raven and her first mate. The three formed a special bond without even trying. Raven had become the leader, Gezana the follower and Lorenzo the caretaker of both.

Without meaning to, Gezana fell for Lorenzo and the feelings were returned. It seemed to have happened overnight, but actually was over many cycles of the moon. It was the little things that brought the love into each other's hearts so that it could bloom into something bigger. Gezana would sit for an hour or more every night discussing whatever came to mind with Lorenzo.

Lorenzo always made sure Gezana had a little larger serving of dinner or an extra biscuit. While the older man was tending to matters on deck, Lorenzo would be in his cabin mending the little tears in Gezana's clothes that he always swore he never knew how they got there.

When they would make port, Gezana always searched for a special item that he knew Lorenzo would like. Whether it be a certain spice that he liked but always seemed to be running out of or one of the rare ones, the younger man cherished them equally.

Many times Lorenzo would get permission from Raven to go to town on his own or with another one of her men as his escort. She didn't like him going alone because his smaller stature and boyish young looks made him a target for some of the men they were liable to run into on the way into town.

It was on those trips that Lorenzo would find special things that he knew Gezana would like. Sometimes it was a pot of honey for his biscuits and other times a special higher quality of whiskey. In the end he always cherished the way Gezana was in awe of his little gifts. It made him feel extremely special and loved that he, a young man who had started as almost a slave upon the ship many years before, was now equal with all the crew and loved completely by one in particular.

What had cemented Gezana's love for Lorenzo had been the two beautiful bowls he had carved from the wood that Gezana had brought him from one such trip.

For Lorenzo, his love for Gezana grew in the same manner. The catalyst had been the finest strips of leather that he had ever seen. Gezana had told him that he bought it for him because he knew he would love it.

As the love between them grew it helped Lorenzo become stronger in all aspects of his life. His confidence blossomed, causing him to hold his head high with pride which carried over to his having the utmost respect for Raven and how she treated everyone as her equal even though she was captain of the ship. In turn, the crew thought of Lorenzo as one of them and gave him as much respect as they did Raven and Gezana. They were equally grateful when he took over most of the cooking. There were some things the cook excelled at and some that weren't fit to feed the sharks. Under Lorenzo's skillful hand, though, the food improved tenfold.

Gezana watched as Lorenzo changed and he couldn't have been prouder. He knew the smaller man would never be as big and muscular as the rest of them, but Lorenzo needed to know how to defend himself. Gezana gradually trained his lover in the use of a dagger and how to protect himself in other ways without using weapons. He didn't even bother to try to teach him how to use a sword, knowing it would be too much for him.

✝

After ten seasons Raven decided they needed a rest. For the next full season, they left their home base only once to obtain supplies. They rested, hunted, and played cards. Over the next twelve moons currency was lost, then gained once more in the next hand.

One afternoon, in the second moon of their rest, Raven sat on the porch of her bungalow watching the sparring competition she convinced them to have. They were rowdy, loud, and drunk. Usually not an ideal combination for pirates, but not one man was hurt. That, in and of itself, astonished her. She thought for sure she was going to see Lorenzo stitching at least one of them.

No blood was drawn...that was until one of the drunken men challenged Raven herself. She tried to convince him he did not want to challenge her, but he was with them only a few moons. He had not fully come to see what Raven was truly capable of doing to a man.

When she was through with him, she'd knocked him down a peg and he had found new respect for the tall, dangerous woman. With the last swing of the sword, Raven had grazed the right side of his face. Sinking his sword in the dirt hilt up, he admitted defeat. In the end, both shared a laugh and a drink, calling it a lesson learned on his part.

The entire crew was loyal to Raven, Gezana, and Lorenzo. Most of the men had been with them since their maiden voyage many long seasons ago. Raven knew without a doubt they would all die for her. She, however, would never ask that of them. When the time came, she knew she would accept her fate and follow whatever god showed up for her, not letting one of them take her place.

†

It was eleven seasons after that fateful night at the castle and Raven's ship was making its way to the eastern colonies. She tied up at Turlan, a port they often stopped at for pleasure.

Once docked, Gezana left the usual three men guarding the ship and went in search of the woman he had found several seasons ago for Raven. She was one of only a few that could quiet the fire burning within the pirate.

He returned with her before Raven was finished with her bath. Wrapped only in her long crimson silk robe Raven entered her cabin from the adjoining one, where she kept her bath and toiletries. Upon seeing the naked woman lounging on her bed, Raven's blood pressure rose and dampness gathered between her thighs. As her ruthlessness on the seas grew, so too had her appetites in the pleasure arena.

After making the wench cry out her name repeatedly, Raven now lounged in her chair. Her silk robe lay beneath her as her right leg was causally thrown over the arm of the chair. The other woman knelt on the floor in front of her with her head between her thighs. Raven's head was thrown over the back of the chair, her back arched in pleasure, lost in the moment barely aware of the goings-on outside.

Raven put her large calloused hand on the back of the woman's head to hold her where she wanted her mouth to be. She groaned in pleasure. Once more on the verge of orgasm, she made her wishes known. "Suck harder…that's it…"

She felt the fire burning through her, the liquid lava flowing freely from her as it started. "Suck it…by the Gods, YES…." The flow that washed through her caused her to rise off the chair, screaming her release. The stupid girl at that moment tried something new to please her. The wench started to penetrate Raven with her fingers, as had been done to herself time and time again.

Raven reacted violently. Standing, she threw the girl across the room. The fury crackled around the pirate like lightning. "I told you NEVER, touch me there! I would easily be within my right to kill you." She advanced on where the woman cowered in fear in the corner of the cabin. She was halfway across the room when her cabin door burst open.

Gezana, with his sword drawn, burst forth. "Capt'n…hurry…pirates attacking the port." Not for a split second did he notice Raven was completely naked, having left her silk robe lying on the chair.

Raven looked at the sobbing creature, then at her first mate. "Damn, we do not have time for this. Gather the men, tell them what is happening." As she dressed, she lecherously addressed the woman. Raven knew she would have need of the woman when she returned. Battle always drove her into a lustful frenzy and it was very rare to have a woman on board to appease her. Usually she had only her own hands to quiet the hunger. This would be a rare treat to have a woman present upon her return. "You! Be here waiting when I get back and maybe I'll forgive you."

†

The captain and her men found the port militia outnumbered and outfought when they arrived. When the fighting was over, all but four of the militia where dead, Raven had lost one of her own and the attackers had run for higher ground.

This time Raven herself did not come out unscathed. One of the pirates had managed to get though her defenses with a dagger.

Having sent the young woman home upon arrival back at her cabin, Raven now drank heavily from the bottle Gezana handed her as Lorenzo prepared to sew up the wound on her face. The pirate had managed to slice the right side of her face from her hairline to her jaw, barely missing her eye.

Wiping away the blood from her face, Lorenzo motioned for Gezana to meet him outside the cabin. In the hall, he told the older man his fears. "Gez, it is deep and bad. I cannot tell what damage has been done; only that it looks to have missed her eye. To work so close to her eye she needs to be out when I stitch. I put something in the rum you gave her. She should be out in no time."

A moment later, they heard the bottle crash to the floor. It took longer than he thought to close the wound, his hand cramping by the time he was done. Lorenzo had made

104

the stitches as small as he could. Raven however was still going to have a powerful scar down the length of her face.

Chapter Six

Several seasons later Raven looked into the oval mirror, finding an unfamiliar face. Yes, it was hers, yet it was not. She had spent since sunrise having the scar covered with an intricate blue and green design. The pattern covered the scar the entire length of her face. The tattoo then wove down the side of her neck onto her shoulder, coming to an end upon her shoulder blade where it met her birthmark; that of which looked like a bird. "Wow! Three seasons have passed since that day on the docks. It seems as if only yesterday."

It was a design she remembered seeing in her youth. However, try as she might, she could not remember where. Since that day in Turlan, her name had become known in all ports. A legend sprouted that day, that it was El Diablo who had saved them and that El Diablo was indeed a woman.

She stood before the mirror, studying the design once more. It was as familiar as her own face. She laughed at that. "I could be a bard...I know this design, Gezana, yet I cannot place it."

Gezana stood in the doorway ready to call to her, when she turned to face him. He thought it strange that she would know the pattern when they had never been to that country from which the design came. This told him something of her past, because in all the seasons they were together she had yet to tell him a thing.

He strode forth as the man who had completed the design left the room. "So I see you have been to Pavlone." Raven spun around and pinned him against the chair. It was not anger that shone in her eyes, but fear.

"Why do you speak that name?"

Never before had he been witness to the terror in her eyes. "That…" he cleared his throat. "That is where that design is from. It is on their coat of arms."

†

Raven stumbled backward. It all came back to her, causing her eyes to slam shut. She found it hard to breathe under the pain of remembering.

It came back to her in a rush…that day, the sun shining, the meadow and the beautiful woman. She could smell her, as if she was standing in front of her. She smelled of roses and honey.

Then the pain in Raven's chest rose, pounding in her ears. "By the Gods…Kat…" She fell against the wall behind her. Then found herself sitting upon the floor. "What have I done, Gezana? What have I done?" He came over and sat beside her. Never before had Raven reacted this way.

As they sat Raven's story poured forth, starting at the beginning, long before she met the other half of her soul. She told him of betrayal, humiliation, and lastly, of how she had loved Kat. She told him of how that love had been her undoing.

†

Gezana's heart broke for the woman she might have been; for the warrior she most certainly would have been, but not for the pirate she had become. Who she had become was not who she was or who she was meant to be. He knew for a fact she did not belong in this life. Gezana knew that now more than ever before.

Over the seasons, he had heard rumors about Pavlone. Most of the stories centered around a princess who had become queen and of a king who was not a king. He heard stories of how females, not the king, graced the queen's bed. However, the rumors he had heard over the last several seasons concerned him the most.

A traveling bard had told tales of a warrior called Dragon and of how he had conquered Pavlone and its surrounding lands. He feared for what had happened to the princess that had surely become queen, for he knew she was Raven's soulmate. If she was lost, then there was no hope in saving his captain.

"I have never felt right about leaving the way I did. I should have stayed and confronted her. Something about that night has never felt right to me. I am sure by now she is happily married, raising many children. I surely cannot go back to her now, even though I have the means to take care of her as she is accustomed to. What else do I have to offer her? Now...I cannot even offer her my name. I am nothing. I am El Diablo." Raven sat upon the floor, head in her hands; the heavy burden of all she left behind crashed in upon her.

Gezana grasped her arm. "You do have something to offer; never have doubt of that. You have yourself to offer. You are worth more than all the gold and gems we have ever touched. Take yourself to her and then you will know.

Raven, you cannot go on as you have. I have watched you over the seasons. As each one passes, you come closer and closer to blackness. Please, my friend, let us sail for Pavlone."

She pulled her arm from his grasp and stood. Her mood had turned, the anger poured from her. "No! What would a murdering pirate have to offer a princess who is now surely a Queen?" Starting for the door of the shop, she was once again stopped by Gezana's hand on her arm.

"Raven, hear me out. I understand now. I..."

Raven held up her hand to stop him. "What Gez...what do you understand? That I am a murderer... a pirate? Or that I am...that I am not worthy of her?" Defeated she threw herself into the chair she had vacated earlier.

"My friend...what I now understand is everything you have done over all these seasons has been for one purpose, to purge yourself of her. It has not worked, has it? Look deep within yourself to find the truth. You survive for one purpose only, to see her once again. Am I not correct?" Crossing his arms, he leaned against the small table in front her.

Never had anyone seen a moment of weakness or fear from her. When she lifted her head to plead with him, tears streamed down her cheeks for the first time in fourteen seasons. "I cannot. What if she shows me only pity? I would rather die than see pity in her eyes."

The emotion in her eyes put more fear in him than any one of the Gods ever could. She would be lost soon if something was not done. "Raven, we set sail for Pavlone. You must trust in the Fates. They will guide you. Why do you think this design in particular came to mind to adorn your scar-covered face? 'Twas the Fates, that is who. They are telling you that you must return to where this all began. That maybe she is in need of you."

Raven learned long ago to trust Gezana's intuition. "In need of me?" She paused, hoping against hope that it was true. "Fine then, my friend, let us set sail for Pavlone. The northern route is in full winter so we will need to travel around the southern cape. Have the crew set sail back the way we came." She threw on her hooded cape preparing to leave the shop.

Gezana relayed information he had heard the previous nightfall. "We will need to be very cautious. I heard tell in the pub last night that a new and dangerous pirate sails these waters. The bard told tales that he more than rivals El Diablo. This new one also attacks ports. I wonder if this is not the same one that scarred you, we met up with them in Turlan and then again in Zien."

Sighing, she patted him on the back. "Then let us be cautious, old friend, so that we may live to see another season. If need be we only sail very slowly by night. As is it, it will take us five moons to get to Pavlone. If we have to travel like this, it will likely take us several more. However, I would like to get there in one piece. I am returning to the ship. You go make sure Lorenzo acquires extra supplies."

Gezana followed her through the doorway. "What shall I tell the crew?"

She thought for a moment. "Tell them what you like, it matters not to me." Upon arrival at her ship, Raven retired to her cabin. She needed to plan, to think on what was needed to accomplish her task.

†

Gezana would wait until they were closer to Pavlone to tell her other stories he had heard. He would tell Raven the tale of the Dragon coming to power and the death of the would-be King Nicholas and Renaldo. Gezana dreaded telling her of the rumors of King Theos and Kataryna, of how they were tortured and discarded. In the meantime, he made all the crew aware to be ever vigilant in their watches. Each crewmember was assigned to keep watch in short shifts, so as not to fall asleep on duty.

Chapter Seven

Raven stood on deck, the rest of the crew skittered about preparing to pull into port by the next nightfall, if all went well. After watching a moment to make sure everything was going smoothly, she gazed back up at the night sky. Gezana quietly walked across the deck and stood behind her.

Even though he did not make a sound, she knew he was there. After all these seasons, she had a knack for feeling things and this was one of them. She could close her eyes and know where each of her crew were and what they were doing.

He silently stood behind her with his hands folded behind his back, watching as she closed her eyes to contemplate her surroundings. In her own time she would acknowledge him. Out of the corners of his eyes, he observed the others moving about. Each of them knew better than to approach Raven when she was in a mood such as this night. The sorry few who had, rapidly learned to never do so again. That was, of course, after they picked themselves up from the ground after the severe beating they took.

The two pirates stood in silence. Raven marveled at what had brought them to this point.

She was working something out in her head, so Gezana stood by his friend and waited. As always, he did not have long to wait. Raven's mind worked faster than any he knew. This was one of the many reasons she was so good in a fight. She was always ten steps ahead of her opponent.

She did not acknowledge his presence in any way. Instead, she voiced what was on her mind, knowing she had his full attention the entire time. Raven leaned her arms on the railing, resting her chin in her hands.

A few more moments passed before she was ready to put words to her thoughts. "It seems I have come back to the beginning. Is it not funny how one's life comes full circle before we know our mistakes?"

Gezana knew better than to answer, he continued to stand silently behind her. "I left here fifteen seasons ago, a brokenhearted young rebel. Now I return a brokenhearted, beaten, old pirate who fears for what has happened to the princess who stole her heart so long ago."

Raven felt his body stiffen slightly. "Yes, old friend, you heard me right. There is something I fear in life. The Gods know I do not fear death. They may take me at any time they wish, but I would have only one regret, that I did not know what has happened to her. Even if I were never to lay eyes upon her, I have the need to know she is safe."

Pulling herself upright, she turned. "From what you have told of, we will have to be swift in obtaining the news that we require. I want to be prepared to leave here quickly if need be. This is one of those times I feel the hairs on the back of my neck standing on end and as if a stone sits at the bottom of my gut."

Gezana moved to stand beside her. "That is never a good sign, Raven. Do you wish for me to alert the crew?"

Raven shook her head, causing her long braid to swing back and forth. "No, I do not want to cause alarm as of yet. Just tell them to be vigilant as always. I also plan on leaving Lorenzo here. I know he will be angry. He will have to live with it."

Gezana knew this was not going to end well. That Raven had suggested leaving Lorenzo behind set off his internal alarms even more. He prayed to whatever Gods were listening that if they were to die now, to make it swift. "I will attend to it, Captain." He stepped away to speak with some of the crew who would be standing watch.

†

Luck had smiled upon them. Not once did they run into trouble along the way. When they were less than half a moon from Pavlone, Raven had Gezana hoist the merchant flag. She wanted no trouble as they entered Pavlone's waters. As they docked Gezana and Lorenzo told Raven of the remainder of what they had heard of the happenings in Pavlone.

Upon hearing that her princess might be in danger, she made the decision she would be the one to lead the group of handpicked men off the ship and into town. This time and in this port, above all others, she wanted her presence known. Raven wanted this Dragon to know that El Diablo had come a calling.

The crew gathered on the deck awaiting orders. The moon was at its highest point in the night sky. It was a full moon and one of the brightest the pirates had seen in many seasons. Most of them thought this was surely a sign, a sign to bring them great wealth.

After fifteen seasons with Raven as their captain, they were as loyal as they had been in the beginning. They would die for her. They would do anything for her, including going into the Dragon's lair to rescue her princess. Gezana had told them when they set sail for Pavlone why they were going there. Some had heard the same bard's stories as he, yet all said 'Aye' and they set sail. There was not one among them who would not battle the Dragon himself, to protect what their captain was after.

As she looked over the crew, she was not so sure of herself. Self-doubt raised its ugly head. Her eyes swept from man to man and finally landed upon Lorenzo. He had grown so much as a person over the seasons, she was very proud of him. It was going to hurt her to tell him he had to stay behind this time. She only wanted to take less than a handful of the crew with her, on the slim chance there was trouble.

Gezana had told her of the bard's stories of the Dragon. One story caught her attention in particular. She now feared for Lorenzo, knowing that he came from Lenara and held the telltale brand on his arm. Raven learned the Dragon had destroyed most of Lorenzo's homeland and any of the men that did not wish to serve in her armies where considered traitors and put to death. Learning this, she did not want him seen in town because of the possibility of being captured.

He would never have made the request, but Gezana was thankful she was leaving him behind. He did not want special treatment for his lover and would never have asked. However, even after all this time he still wanted to look out for Lorenzo, to care for him. So, fearing that harm might come to him because Lorenzo was from Lenara scared him more than he wanted to admit.

The dockmaster stood waiting for the plank to be lowered so he could board and collect the tariffs due. She addressed her men. "Gezana, I will deal with the dockmaster. You prepare three men to go to town with us. Lorenzo you will stay with the ship."

She saw the hurt in his eyes. "No argument this time. I wish to test the waters before I chance any of the rest of you getting off this ship. It may or may not be safe for us to dock here and I do not wish to risk it." She flipped the hood on her cloak up to cover her head and face so only part of her facial features could be seen. Her black braid snaked over her shoulder and down her chest, as if protecting her.

✝

Raven did not want the dockmaster on board her ship; instead, she strolled down the plank to meet him on his own dock. She knew how this would be perceived, yet she did not care. She trusted no one to board her ship except her own men.

"My good man, we wish to dock here for the night. With whom do we register?" She grinned knowing he was the dockmaster and would tell her so.

He looked her over from her black leather boots to her hood-covered head leering the whole time. He found this woman's voice intoxicating. "Your captain may pay me the docking tariff and you may dine with me this evening."

Raven shifted only her eyes to Gezana, who had now joined her. She chuckled and then her eyes landed once more on the shorter man. Behind her, she heard the gasp of her men. "Little man, you are speaking to the captain of this vessel and do not dare presume I would have anything else to do with you. What is this tariff you speak of?"

He looked upon her once more with doubt in his eyes. The short, smelly man tried once more to see under the hood she wore. "You are the captain of this ship? I know of only three female captains of merchant ships and those belong to Pavlone and her sister cities. Do you hail from one of those?"

He was testing her. "I hail from the east. That is all you need know, my good man. Now, what of this tariff you speak of?" Raven put her hand on the hilt of her sword and waited.

"'Tis twenty gold pieces and it is the tariff for docking at the Dragon's docks. If you wish not to pay the tariff, go back to sea." He waited expectantly while eyeing her sword.

She pulled a pouch from under her tunic and flipped him something even better. He looked down and in his hand were the two largest rubies he had ever seen.

His eyes widened and he sucked in his breath. He could not fully see her, but he had heard of her beauty as well as her fury. He now knew who she was. She was the pirate known as El Diablo. The dockmaster knew he wanted to be on her good side in order to acquire more of these gems.

Yet he knew something more, he knew the sword. It was unique. He had only ever seen one like it before and that was many, many seasons before. "You may dock here as long as you wish. Please enjoy the taverns; they have all that you seek if you are to ask the right questions." He turned, gone in an instant, his coat billowing behind him. He did not want to be in her presence when the trouble started. Trouble, he knew, would find her; it was only a matter of time.

Raven pulled the hood and cloak tighter around her. "Well, I guess it is to the taverns then. Lorenzo, let no one board my ship. Gezana, lead on."

†

Raven noticed one thing in particular as they made their way through the streets. All of the guards they had come across were women. She thought that strange. When she had been there last there were no women among the guards or the palace troops.

She was not the only to take notice. So did Gezana. He had a tickling in the back of his mind and it was not good. Not once had any of the bards told of what had happened to the princess. Now he feared the worst.

Gezana's mind raced. What if? No, it could not be! It would destroy Raven!

"Gez is something strange and out of place here, or is it me?" She kept her voice down so as not to alert the others with them.

"Aye, I see it too. Be alert, my friend." He moved his hand to the hilt of his sword.

They approached the tavern, Gezana entering first. Raven and the others followed, securing a table in the back. Gezana ordered all of them meals and ale from the barkeep then joined them at the table.

Keeping her hood in place, Raven sat at the corner of the table out of the way. From her vantage point, she could keep an eye on everyone in the tavern, just as Gezana could watch the front and back doors from his.

After their meals were consumed, replenishment ales were ordered. The barkeep approached their table slowly. The dockmaster had come in the back way as they ate and told his brother, the tavern owner, that a ship had docked and that they might make their way to his tavern. He, however, did not tell him whose ship it was. Setting the fresh ales down, he addressed Gezana, "Do you wish accommodations for the night?"

No one spoke. The barkeep cleared his throat, "I only ask because I only have two rooms empty. Will you be wishing them, Captain?"

When still no one answered a hush fell over the tavern. Raven kept her head down as if looking at the floor. She let Gezana play him along for another few moments.

Gezana addressed the barkeeper. "Tell me barkeep, what of King Theos?"

The man looked at the Gezana, assuming he was the captain and took a step back. That was one of the names no one spoke aloud; he looked around. Bending over so only Gezana could hear him, "Be careful, Captain. There are things no one speaks of any longer in Pavlone."

†

Raven pounded her fist upon the table. "Enough! Barkeep, if you wish to address the one in charge it will be me and answer my good friend's question." Raven raised her head, still not pulling the cloak from her head.

He glared at her. "Who be you then?"

"I be the captain. That is who! Tell me...what has happened to King Theos and Princess Kataryna?"

The barkeep looked horrified. "Shh....do not speak those names aloud."

Pulling the hood back, the captain looked up at him. He gasped when he saw her face. She was the one. The one the elders had foretold, the one with the marking. He sat and

119

quietly told the tales, as he knew them. He told of the Dragon rising from the depths of Hades and sweeping across the lands conquering all in its path. He told of the banishment of King Theos to the outlands where it was rumored he still survived. As for Princess Kataryna, no one knew for sure what had happened to her. Upon finishing, he bowed his head.

Raven had a final question. "What happened to Lord Renaldo?"

The tavern owner laughed a cruel laugh, he had never liked the man to begin with. "The Dragon sent him to Hades not long after sending King Nicholas to his grave as well."

As he stood, he delivered a parting word of advice, even though she was the one foretold. "If you wish to live another sunrise you should return to your ship, set sail and never look back. The Dragon, she brings only death and destruction upon others, as do her children who fight by her side. She returns before the next nightfall from Citrin."

After he disappeared into the back, they noticed they were completely alone in the tavern. Gezana's worst fears where confirmed. He knew what had happened to Raven's princess, she was none other than the Dragon herself. Fear washed through him for her soul. What would become of her when she found out?

One of the keeper's daughters came to clear the table. While removing the dishes in front of Raven she smiled, accidentally brushing her breast against Raven's shoulder sending Raven's libido soaring. Just as fast it crashed, when she remembered why she was here.

Gezana waited until the girl had left to speak. "Raven, I think it is best if we return to the ship for the night."

"Yes, let's return here in the morning. I wish an audience alone in the morning with this Dragon. I want to know what has happened to the princess. Let us take our leave of this place."

"Raven, maybe we should heed the barkeep. Keep in mind Lenara is part of the Dragon's kingdom. I am sure if any of her troops made it back, they told her of running into us." Gezana was concerned they would wear out their welcome at the dock before sunrise.

"Gez, that was seasons ago that we ran into them. Surely, the Dragon or her troops would not be bothered with us. I really do not see where we would be much of a threat. Besides that, we have never attacked any port or city, unlike what we have heard about her. No, I really do not see an issue with that. I, however, do want to know where the princess is. So help me, by the Gods, she better be unharmed." The growl came from deep in Raven's soul.

"Could it be you still love her?" Gezana chuckled as he stood.

†

Raven pretended to contemplate her answer for a moment. She truly was not sure how she felt. "I think not, yet I want nothing bad to happen to her. I am past wishing her ill." She returned the hood to her head before leaving the tavern. They exited the front door, turning the corner toward the docks. Raven could hear footsteps behind them. She motioned for Gezana to continue while she turned right onto one of the side streets. As she predicted they followed her, not her men.

At the next side street, Raven turned the corner sharply and hid in one of the doorways. The footsteps raced past her as she grasped the person's arm. She pulled the smaller body to hers and whispered in her ear. "Do you wish to dance with El Diablo, little girl?"

Raven had known it was the girl from the tavern following them. The girl was young but still old enough to know better than to follow a pirate into the night. Raven thought her to be at least seventeen seasons old. She wanted to put the fear of the gods in her. "Well, little one? Why do you follow me?"

The girl shook with fear, yet also with excitement. "My uncle owns a merchant ship that has been to many of the same ports as you and has told me stories of El Diablo upon his return. Please let me explain. Do not take lightly what my father tells you. Please take your ship and leave. To stay here will only be your destruction. Please leave while you can."

Raven wrapped her arms around the girl and kissed her neck. She put her lips on her ear and whispered, "Do you not fear me, little one?"

She leaned into the warmth. "No, my Captain, but I do fear her and her children. She rules over all the lands and any that do not see as she does, well...let us say they no longer see. So please, return to your ship and go."

Raven brought her right hand up, covering the girl's right breast. She squeezed and felt her nipple harden. "Tell me, little one, what has happened to *my Princess Kataryna?*" Squeezing again, she was rewarded with a moan.

The young barmaid felt a moment of jealousy when the pirate called the princess hers. "No one knows. Some say she is held within the dungeons and others say she is dead by her own hand. All say the Dragon had her way with her before her disappearance. I do not think you would want to claim her as yours after the Dragon was through with her.

Besides, she would be too old for you now. I would think you would like someone younger. Please, my Captain..." The captain squeezed again, let go of her and turned to leave. "Please I..."

Raven heard the wanting in her voice. She turned back toward the girl, pinned her roughly against the wall and gave her more than what she wanted. Raven walked away chuckling a few moments later, as the sobbing girl slid to the cobblestones because her legs could no longer hold her up. The look on the girl's face as she entered her told Raven that she was a virgin. It was confirmed a heartbeat later as she felt the telltale membrane tear under the thrusting of her fingers.

She gazed back at her once more. "Tell me, little one, who is the one to be feared now?"

"I could never fear you, *my Captain*. If you have need of me, you know where to find me. As for your Princess, she still resides in the palace."

The way the young girl spoke Raven's title sent shivers up her spine. Another had fallen prey to her charms, this time though it held no thrill for her.

✝

All the girl had wanted was to be kissed; instead, she received an awakening. She now knew it was not a man she wanted to grace her bed, but a woman. Even though this dangerous woman had taken her roughly and with no care for her feelings, she would let her do it again, if the captain so chose to. She had fallen for El Diablo with the first touch, just as so many others had over the years.

✝

Raven made her way back to her ship as fast as she could. After the first street, she realized it must have been very late as she found the streets deserted. In the distance she heard what she thought were a herd of hoofbeats. She knew it was either an advance party of the Dragon's guards or the Dragon herself.

Startled into awareness she picked up the pace and broke into a run, wanting to get back to the ship unrecognized. Why take the chance before she could find the princess? As her legs picked up the pace so did her conscience. By the time she arrived at her ship, guilt had taken its toll on her. She was a wreck. Why had she had her way with the young girl? Was she not in search of Kataryna?

Gezana stood on deck awaiting her return. She ran up the plank, past him to the barrel of water. He watched as she scrubbed her hands and face as if trying to wash away something truly foul. She turned back to him, the guilt clearly on her face. "Ah...and now you feel guilt. Why do you feel as such? Could it be you still feel something for the princess?" He shook his head. He had known who was following them, what Raven would do, and he even knew the guilt she would feel.

There was no doubt in Gezana's mind that she still loved Kataryna. Her actions told him she would do anything to find her or she would die trying. He dared not tell her his conclusion that the princess and the Dragon were the same being. More information was needed before he would do such a thing.

Raven leaned against the railing and looked out over the bay as she spoke to Gezana. "The girl did have one interesting thing to say. She says the princess still lives in the castle. Do not worry. I heard your question; I am just thinking things out. Upon further reflection, you should go to the palace with me. We will leave in a couple of hours. Why don't you go get some sleep, I am sure Lorenzo is worried."

Gezana smiled.

"Ah, you already checked in with him." Not able to contain it, she roared with laughter. "You, my good man, are so whipped! Go! Remember I want to be at the palace at sunrise."

She remained a few moments longer, deep in thought. She spoke to no one but the murky waters of the bay. "Kat, what has become of you? I feel I am missing something. Please, by the Gods, let you not be harmed."

After a shake of her head, she made her way to her cabin for a few hours of rest. "Something is out of place and I cannot put my finger on it."

✝

As Raven strolled about the deck the next morning, checking in with her crew, Gezana told Lorenzo what they had learned. He then spoke his worst fears. He told Lorenzo he feared Raven's princess and the Dragon were one and the same.

Lorenzo sat up in their bunk, despair clearly written on his face. "Gez...it will destroy her. She tries so hard to hide it. None see it but you and I...she still loves the princess. What will we do? She is on the edge of the abyss and this will send her over."

"Yes, but in what direction? Will she give herself completely to her darker self or will she fight to bring back her beloved?" He pulled Lorenzo back down upon the bed beside him.

Lorenzo sighed and committed himself to helping her. "I will not let her be lost. She had faith in me. Now I have it in her."

Gezana lightly caressed the side of his face. "So do I love…so do I. We will not let her falter."

Chapter Eight

Moments before the sun crested the horizon, Raven and Gezana made their way through town. As they walked the streets, Raven took in the differences from fifteen seasons before. Dread set in.

Gone were the carts that packed the streets selling baked goods, meats, and wares. Now there only remained a handful. She looked over the food items for sale; they looked to be old and withered. She saw no carts selling wares whatsoever. Raven had a sinking feeling in the pit of her stomach.

She stopped in her tracks, did a full turn around, coming to a stop staring back down the way they were headed. Another observation had hit her. There were no children running and playing in the streets.

Many seasons ago, mere moments before dawn there had been dozens of children. Some were playing games, some running from vendor to vendor to look at the goodies, and some helping their parents with their carts.

Now there were none. She saw not one single child. She saw no happiness, no...no something. She could not quite put her finger on it at first. Then it hit her and what heart she had left cried for them. "Living…that is what is missing. These people are merely existing. They fear for their lives and for the lives of their children." It was hitting her how miserable and beaten down these people were.

Gezana stood by and watched the anguish wash over her.

She turned and looked at him. "Gez, I have done many things over the seasons, very bad things, but I do not think I have ever been the cause of this. Have I? Have I decimated like this?" Her sorrow and grief emanated from her.

"No Raven, you have never been the cause of such utter destruction. I see no hope in their faces. No hope of a future."

Raven approached one of the vendors. He rapidly backed away.

"Please, my Lord, what I have is yours."

She looked at Gezana and saw he too was puzzled. "My good man, I am not your Lord, I am not even from here. I have no need of your items this morning and I have no wish to take anything without paying for it. What I am in need of is information." She pulled the hood of her cloak back a little, so he could get a good look at her face.

The merchant backed away even further in fear; fear for his life. "You are one of her demons, do as you wish; I have nothing more to offer. She has already taken all of my best crops, just as she took my daughter last season. I have nothing left to offer her, except my life."

Raven stepped closer. "My good man, I have no wish to take your life. As I told you, I am not from here. I am from the east. Tell me who you fear so much?" She stepped closer to him.

A passing merchant joined them. He took one look at her face and knew exactly whom she was. "I saw you in the tavern last nightfall. I heard the things you ask. You do not belong here. You must go. You will bring death to all that are near you if you continue. Please take your leave of Pavlone, before you get us all killed." The merchant went back to his cart, pushing it away as fast as he could, leaving the other merchant to fend for himself.

She turned from watching the man scurry away to address the remaining merchant. "Tell me, my good man, should I heed his warning and leave?"

He stared into her eyes, summoning his courage. "Aye, you should. There is nothing but death here for you. Please take what you want and leave."

"As I said, I wish no food this morning. What I want is information. When I last was in your city, the streets were lined with carts, brimming with the finest food and wares I have ever seen. There were also children running about. Now there are none."

He lowered his head in grief. "My Lord, those who have them keep the boys inside and now send the girls as far away as they can. As for the food and wares, all the best goes to the palace. We are left with...well you see what we are left with." His hand swept over his meager offerings.

Raven's anger flared. "How could this have happened? What has this Dragon done to these people? Gezana, let us be on our way." Before she left, Raven slipped the merchant a few coins from her pouch.

Her fears of what had happened to the princess and King Theos resurfaced. "I feel sorry for these people. They were happy under King Theos's rule. He must never have stood a chance against her of being conquered. Her armies

129

must have marched through these lands like a plague. By the Gods, what has happened to Kataryna?"

✝

En route to the palace Raven changed their plans once more. She would remain behind at the tavern while Gezana continued ahead to request an audience with the Dragon. Something told her to keep the knowledge of her existence quiet for the moment.

They stopped at the tavern door. Gezana stood with his hand on his sword. "I will continue to the palace as planned. Try not to cause any trouble while I am gone."

Raven laughed. "I do not cause it, it just follows. Be careful my friend. We know not what lies at the palace. I will await your return here."

He took her arm. "You be careful as well, my friend. I want you in one piece when I return."

Raven turned and entered the tavern, not wanting to watch him continue without her. She still was unsure if it was a good idea for him to go alone. The tavern owner and his family were having their morning meal. She was not surprised to find the tavern door open. The owner was a good man and welcomed all; he had proven that the night before, when instead of warning her he could have called the guards.

She moved past the empty tables in the front to one in the back corner. A moment after sitting, a bowl containing a delicious-smelling porridge and plate of bread were placed on the table in front of her. She looked up to see the young girl from the night before.

The girl smiled down at her and brushed her fingers over the back of Raven's hand. "I thought you might be

130

hungry, Captain. If you have further need of me, please call for me. My name is Myra."

Raven smiled back at her, noticing the flirting. She however would not repeat last night's mistake. "Thank you, Myra. This will be more than enough. Tell your father thank you for being so kind." She withdrew several coins and put them in Myra's hand.

Knowing enough to take the subtle hint that her advances would not be welcome, Myra withdrew and went back to the kitchen.

Raven finished her meal as the girl's father approached. "Please sit," Raven gestured, "the meal was wonderful. Tell your wife for me. If I may, I'd like to stay here until my friend returns?"

He sat and studied her. "You may stay, since I see you did not heed my warning."

"I apologize, but I could not leave. I am here to see an old friend. While I wait for Gezana to return, I would like you to tell me what the Dragon looks like."

The barkeep's daughter, upon arriving home the previous evening, told him of the questions the woman had asked of her. He was one of the few left that remembered the reigning days of King Theos. He also was one of the few who knew who the Dragon really was. The tavern owner could tell her all he knew, but to what end. What good would it do to tell her now, when she was planning on going to the palace? She would find out soon enough for herself.

"There are some questions that should remain unanswered. If you intend to go to the palace you will find out for yourself soon enough. The answers you seek returned this dawn." The owner stood as to leave. "If you wish, I will have Myra bring you more food and drink."

Raven knew enough not to push the issue. It was now more obvious than even before, that something was very wrong in Pavlone. She would find out shortly just what it was when she met with the Dragon. "Yes, that would be good. Thank you for your hospitality."

†

Gezana, much to his surprise, received a warm welcome at the palace. He was further astonished when it was one of the Dragon's children he met with. He looked upon her daughter, Bryanne, with amazement; she looked exactly how Raven had described Kataryna.

Before leaving the ship, Lorenzo snuck into Raven's cabin and took the petite chest of jewels from where Raven kept them hidden, thinking no one knew about them. Lorenzo gave them to Gezana.

The first several seasons Raven took the chest out regularly, opening it and gazing at the gems within, losing herself in the past. As the seasons passed, she could no longer remember as clearly, until several seasons had now passed and she had forgotten about the chest. Lorenzo and Gezana both knew who she kept them for, even though she herself did not.

Gezana took the chest with him to the palace to use as a gift for the Dragon. Before leaving the ship, he had once more opened them and gazed at the note inside.

Bryanne stood before Gezana and inspected him. She knew him to be a pirate even though they flew the merchant flag; that much she had been informed of before he arrived at the palace. "I am Captain Bryanne, Captain of the Guards. What brings you to the palace of the Dragon?"

He pulled the small box from under his cloak. "I bring these as a gift to the Dragon from the captain. They are the rarest of diamonds." Yes, he knew exactly whom they were meant for as he watched her daughter open the chest. The black eyes that looked upon the gems and then at him were the same as had been told to him.

"Dragon will be pleased. Never before have we seen such gems. You say these are diamonds. They indeed must be rare. Have you come for an audience with my mother then?" She closed the chest, puzzled by the words on the parchment contained within.

"No, it is not I, Gezana, but my captain that wishes the audience, if it pleases the Dragon." Being somewhat nervous now, waiting to see in what direction fate would take him, he found himself standing at attention.

A puzzled Bryanne turned to leave the room. "Please remain here. I will return shortly." She quickly left the room, informing the guard in the hallway not to let anyone in or out of the room. She rapidly went to her mother's quarters, where she knew she was bathing. They had returned home before dawn that very morning from several moon's travel in the northwest, where they had been called to quell an uprising in Baul.

†

The Dragon soaked in the hot bath water in hopes of soaking off more than the dirt that had seeped into every pore. For the first time in many, many seasons, she wanted to be Kataryna again. Upon leaving Baul, she felt something had changed in her. The battle had taken something from her. Never before had she had to go up against mere children among the dissidents.

133

For the first time since the Dragon emerged, she felt very tired. There had to be an end somewhere to the uprisings, instead there seemed to be at least three every season now. "Damn…Father never had entire countries go against him. Damn, why do they hate me so?" She did not need ask herself the question, for she already knew the answer. She was the Dragon…she was feared, she was hated; never was she loved, only by her children. Even then, they held a hint of fear of her in them, for she had been known to take them to task over their mistakes.

She laid her head back upon the tub and closed her eyes. "Tell me, Fates, where did it all go wrong? How did we end up in these roles? What is our true purpose in all this bloodshed? God of War, I am weary. I have seen too much fighting. I have been the cause of so much loss. I beg of thee, I want it to end. I would do anything for…"

A knock on the door interrupted her thoughts. "Enter."

Bryanne entered carrying a small chest, which she set on the edge of the tub. "Mother, a representative of the ship that docked last nightfall has come bearing this gift and a message from the captain wishing for an audience with you. I cannot be sure but, I feel they may be pirates."

Kataryna opened the chest, picking up one of the gems. "What are these? They are beautiful."

"He says they are black diamonds, the rarest of gems. I remember hearing of such a thing several seasons ago, but I thought they were just a myth. They are as black as our eyes, did you notice? There is a note with them." She carefully watched the expression on her mother's face.

Kataryna dried her hands before picking up the parchment. She opened the paper and read the words. She then reread them a second time. She gazed out the window next to the tub to the blue sky. They touched something in her, something long since lost. She once again read the words.

As I Promised, I Give You the World.

"Who...I cannot remember..." She knew the words from long ago, from the furthest parts of her mind. She could not remember who had spoken them though. "Damn, I cannot remember..." After another moment's thought, she put the paper back into the chest and closed it. "Send a message to this captain, I will meet with him. Tell him after the morning meal though, I wish to contemplate this further."

Knowing a dismissal when it was presented Bryanne bowed and left. She returned to the room she had left Gezana in. "You are in luck today, she will grant your captain his wish. She will meet with him after morning meal."

Gezana bowed his head in respect. "Thank you, I will inform the captain at once." He backed up as to leave.

"Before you go, I have but a question or two about your leader. Where does he hail from originally? Has he been to Pavlone before? Does he wish to trade any wares with Pavlone? Also, what is his purpose here?" She did not want to outright ask his name, for there was something about this that alarmed her, yet intrigued her at the same time. She stood with her hand on her sword belt, waiting for an answer.

†

Gezana had wanted to retreat from the palace as fast a possible before any questions were asked of him; unfortunately, that was not to happen. He would have to evade as many questions as he could. He prayed that she would not ask a name. She had him flustered and he answered as fast as he could, not realizing until too late what he had let slip. "North of Baul originally, I think. That I am not sure of, you would have to ask her. Yes, we have items to trade if you so wish, that and provisions is our purpose here."

Bryanne smiled, she had her answer.

He could not take it back, it was too late. She had caught his slip of the tongue. He now wished it would not be his undoing and he would not lose his life as a result. "I must return to my ship. I beg you good day, Captain Bryanne."

Gezana moved as fast as he could through the streets to the tavern. He now knew for sure that the Dragon and Raven's Kataryna were one and the same. He prayed to the Gods that the guard would not report to her mother what she had learned. He entered the tavern to find Raven relaxing in front of the fire as she drank from a tankard.

He told her of his meeting with the captain of the guards, who in turn was the Dragon's daughter. Gezana informed her she was to meet with the Dragon after the morning meal and that she had better be on her way to the palace if she was to be on time.

✝

Raven made her way slowly to the palace, contemplating every move she would make to obtain the information she needed. While she made her way to the palace, unbeknownst to her, a flurry of activity was setting the halls on fire in the palace.

✝

Bryanne searched the palace for her brother. She tore up and down the halls at a furious pace; knocking over guards, a palace messenger, and Sairana along the way. She finally found Aiden eating in the kitchen. She informed him of all that had occurred; right down to the wording of the note. "I tell you, he said 'her.' The captain of the ship is a woman, a woman pirate nonetheless. The note in the chest sent Mother into a tizzy. Something is going on here. I am worried."

Aiden was her twin in every way. She needed not finish her sentences because he would usually do it for her. They were not only identical looking, their thoughts were similar as well.

Aiden put down the piece of honey-covered bread he had taken a bite of and looked up at her, deep in thought. "I've heard of a female pirate before, but never before has she traveled this far south or even to this part of the seas for that matter. This is very interesting. You say Mother is meeting with her after morning meal? Well, I think we shall be there as well."

Amara, their younger sister, floated into the kitchen. She knew. She had witnessed the coming in her dreams. She came to stand in front of her older siblings. Amara looked at both, yet at nothing. Bryanne, just like her mother, had problems looking Amara in the eyes. Her eyes were like none of theirs. They were so crystal-clear you could look right into the depths of her soul.

"The one we have been awaiting has arrived." She then turned and left the room, leaving the two more puzzled than before her arrival.

It was then that Bryanne remembered Amara's words from the evening before. They had been riding at a steady pace on the last leg of the journey back from Baul, when they stopped for a break. Amara had been more distant than usual in the last several moons and the other two siblings had noticed.

"Amara, is there something wrong? Something we should inform Mother of?" Bryanne was nervous, knowing her sister was a seer.

Amara remounted her horse, turned in the saddle to look at Bryanne and then looked off toward Pavlone. "She has come."

†

Raven arrived at the palace where a guard escorted her to the banquet room. She stood behind the tall ornate oak chair at the end of the table. She noticed there was no chair at the opposite end of the table. This was the Dragon's chair, without a doubt.

The heavy oak door opened behind her. Turning, she found herself face-to-face with a replica of Kataryna when they had first met. All plans she had formulated that morning evaded her. Raven took a step back, not knowing what to make of this. The pirate's mind reeled. "Why…what? By the Gods, what is going on here…"

Bryanne was curious as to the startled response. She also noticed the captain had the hood of her cloak still over her head, making it impossible for anyone to see her face. "I am Bryanne, Captain of the Guards. Could you please lower your hood so I know whom I am addressing?" There was no malice in her voice, only curiosity. She did not want a confrontation with the captain before learning more.

Raven raised her hand to the edge of her hood. "If I might ask of a favor in this matter, may the hood remain? It has been many seasons since any other than my crew has laid eyes upon me. Most would not look kindly upon a female captain of a ship or to....or to look upon my mauled face. Some might look upon a face such as mine with horror and pity. I wish neither. I have earned these scars I carry, just as I have earned the name I carry."

Bryanne spoke without thought, "Much less a pirate captain, El Diablo."

Raven took several nervous steps away from her. "I..." Slipping her hand to her sword.

Bryanne spoke quickly, "I am sorry if I have offended you. I beg your pardon. I meant no offense."

"Accepted...I did not think there was knowledge of who we were; who I am. We are very careful not to let it be known. For the record, harm has never come to any port we have docked at." Raven's body was now on full alert, as was Bryanne's.

Bryanne then remembered what Amara had said... 'She has come.' She then knew; this pirate captain was the one foretold by Amara. Was she the one to save their mother? Was she the one to bring about the downfall of the Dragon? Over the seasons, it had come to be thought there would come two separate beings. Now she was not so sure. It was then that she decided to take a chance and place her trust in the woman. "Please follow me."

Making their way down the hall, Raven studied the young woman walking beside her. She still could not believe her eyes. She looked just as Kat had so many seasons ago, yet she acted nothing like her. What she noticed most was that Bryanne was more confident in herself than Kataryna had been at that age.

They arrived at another large oak door, where Aiden stood waiting for them. "This is my brother Aiden, he is Captain of the Scouts-Archers. This is...is the captain who is here to meet with Dragon."

Raven looked between the two of them, realizing they were twins.

Aiden extended his arm in greeting. "I have heard much about a female pirate, might you be one and the same?" He gave Bryanne a look, silently questioning the hood still in place. She shook her head 'no' and he said nothing about it.

Raven slowly grasped his arm, not knowing if she was in danger or not. For the first time in her life her senses were telling her nothing. "I am one and the same."

She pulled her cloak back a little, to show she came armed and prepared. She wanted there to be no misunderstandings. If need be she would defend herself.

He smiled. "Then I know we have nothing to fear from you. I have never heard of you attacking on land or port. So I bid you welcome to Pavlone."

Aiden stepped forward and opened the door. "This is the war room and you are expected."

As the door opened inward, the three stepped into the room. There, standing at the other end of the room, were the Dragon and Amara.

†

As the trio entered, the Dragon was once more in place, leaving Kataryna in the bath water. Immediately her eyes went to the hilt of the sword hanging at the pirate's side. That sword, a panther's head, she knew it. Her eyes moved further up and she was instantly aware it was a female, not a male pirate.

At the same moment in time, Raven entered the room and set eyes upon Dragon for the first time. Her gasp was loud and she could not stop the words from tumbling from her lips. "No, it cannot be...it cannot. *My Kataryna*, it cannot." A flood of emotions struck her and she stumbled backward.

Dragon stepped forward, going for her sword at the same time. "Pull back your hood, pirate, so that I may see your face and do it NOW!"

Raven hesitated but knew there was no choice. Anger warred with hopelessness within her as she pulled back the hood.

✝

Upon seeing the markings on her face and neck, Bryanne and Aiden drew their swords. It was she; the one that would bring about the downfall of the Dragon. She was now in their presence and they could destroy her, as their mother wanted, but did they want to?

No, they did not. They each truly wanted an end to the battles, to the endless loss of life. They too were tired. They wanted to know the woman who was their mother before she became the 'Dragon.' Bryanne and Aiden wanted a life without bloodshed.

Over the seasons the twin siblings felt their souls stained with the blood of the lives they took. There had to be another way, they knew it was just a matter of finding it. Bryanne grew tired of the villagers cowering in fear every time she rode past them. Aiden, in turn, knew neither of them stood a chance of finding someone to love either of them. So therefore they were destined to rule without love, without heirs.

✝

Before she knew it, the old Kataryna was back, the one lacking in confidence, the one lacking in grace. She stood so stunned she could not move as tears filled the corners of her eyes. Suddenly it became clear to her children that she knew the woman.

Amara stepped between her older siblings and Raven. "NO!" Never before had Amara raised her voice. They were all shocked back to the moment. "She will cause no harm. She is the one. Do not fear her, Mother." She joined her brother and sister, behind Raven.

Her body rigid, Kataryna asked what they all wanted to know. "Why have you returned after all these seasons, Raven? Why?" Silence greeted her. Kataryna took another step closer to her. "You are a pirate, why? Why that? Why return here? Why the black diamonds? Damn you! Tell me what I need to know!"

This time, it was Raven, who took a step closer. "Seasons ago I had forgotten why, yet now I remember as if it was just yesterday's dawn. I met a young girl who I gave my soul and my heart to willingly. She was beautiful, innocent, naïve, and worth moving the heavens for.

"I would have given her all I had without reservation. Yet, I had nothing. When we parted that evening in the hallway, I had planned to tell her the following sunrise that I would return for her, once I had the means to care for her. I felt in my heart that she felt the same for me, as she had told me as such. Much to my surprise, that was not to be. I was informed by another that…that she did not want me, that she asked for me to go away from here." Raven faltered for a split moment in time. "I ached more than I ever thought I could. Not until several moons ago did I come to realize that all I have done over the last fifteen seasons, I have done for her. The wealth is hers as is the heartache and lives I have taken over the seasons. She stole the love I felt and destroyed my soul as well."

Raven closed her eyes for a moment. She remembered the intoxicating scent; it was the same as the first time they were together so long ago. They had just met back up for dinner after bathing and Kat smelled of cinnamon and apples.

The smell took her back to the beginning. To the reason why she became who she was. "What I became, I became for her. I became because of her...As for the gems, they are the rarest of the rare. Only she surpasses their beauty. I obtained them for her many seasons ago." Raven knew then that Gezana must have taken them from her cabin, knowing all along whom they were intended for. By the Gods, he knew! She decided she would deal with him later. She pushed her anger at him aside for the moment.

Raven fought the tears that wanted to flow. "I have thought over the last two seasons that maybe it would have been for the best if the blade that was set upon my face under this ink should not have taken my life instead." Raven lowered her head and set her eyes upon the floor. "Now I am sure it should have."

†

Kataryna was enraged. "I know not what you talk of, you were never sent away. Do not lie!"

Raven raised her head and their eyes met. "I do not lie! I have never lied!"

This angered Kataryna further. "Get out! Get off my lands! Go back to your ship and set sail by sunrise. You, Raven, are not wanted here and if you are not gone by sunrise, I will take offense. Get out now!" Kataryna was bellowing by the time she was finished.

Raven turned to leave, but Kataryna was not finished. "If you had truly loved me, you would never have left. You would have stayed and fought for me. You also would never have become a pirate, one of the lowest life forms. You say it was I who sent you away, I would never have sent you away. I wanted to leave with you, do you not remember?"

It was then that life came full circle and crashed down upon her. Raven knew then that she had been truly duped so many seasons ago. She realized Renaldo had not wanted her there. It was he who had truly sent her away, not her love. What made it worse, she realized, was she had had no faith in the woman who held her heart. "My life is yours to command and I beg your forgiveness at believing another's lies." Raven felt the shame through to her core. She turned to face each of the children. "I am also truly sorry that I am not who you thought I should be." She left, never looking back.

Kataryna stormed out the door behind her and went in the opposite direction to her chambers. She left behind three bewildered children.

It went nothing as Amara knew it should have. Pride had taken over and ruled the day, now all was not as it should have been. "Bryanne, Aiden we must go talk with Raven. We must learn of whom she speaks. We must learn what happened that evening. Come! We must hurry before all is lost."

They hurried in hopes of catching Raven before she made it back to her ship. Amara told them if she made it that far, they might not be able to speak with the captain as her crew may stop them.

The three did not catch up to her as she rapidly made her way through the streets. Raven arrived back at her ship in record time and sent one of her men to bring back Gezana from the tavern where she had told him to wait for her.

†

Raven went to the cabin that had come to be known as her strategy room. There she lost the last shreds of her control. Her mood was darker than she had ever known before in her life. She felt the darkness and anger descend over her. Raven asked herself repeatedly, *"How could I have been so foolish to have hoped for so much?"*

Upon arriving at the ship, Lorenzo told Gezana he was needed in the strategy room immediately, fearing Raven would do herself harm. Even before opening the door, he heard items being thrown against the walls; the sounds of destruction were deafening. When finally there was a lull in the noise, he opened the door.

Raven stood with her back to him, the room was in tatters. "I know it is you, Gez. Do not come in here if you wish to leave with your life. I warn you, I am beyond reason or hope. You should leave when given the chance. I cannot be responsible for my actions."

"No, my friend, I will not. I will not leave you here to wallow in self-pity. Who are we to say her life and yours would be any different than they are now? Perhaps they would have traveled the same course. As you have said, you had planned on leaving that morning anyway. Only the Fates know and they have brought you here this day." He heard a commotion on deck and he had a very good idea who was causing it.

"I will be back. This conversation is not over." When he stepped into the passageway, he found Lorenzo waiting there. Closing the door behind him, Gezana addressed him.

145

"Do not let her out of here. If she means to leave, go with her, no matter where she is headed."

He nodded. "I understand. I will not fail."

Gezana arrived to find Bryanne and two others he did not know standing on the deck, fighting off the crew. "Stand down! Back to work. All of you, NOW!"

He addressed the three. "Why are you here? Has your family not done enough to her? Do you now wish a pound of flesh as well? Perhaps you wish to see her further degraded."

Amara stepped forward. "Tell us, did you know who our mother was before you arrived? Yes, you knew, yet you let Raven come here without telling her. Why did you do that? Did you wish to see her hurt? Why not give her warning?"

"I have no excuse for what I have done. I do wish now that I had told her. At the very least, it would have prepared her for the blackness she now carries. Please excuse me while I go below and try to reason with her." Once at Raven's door, he sent Lorenzo up top to bring the trio down in a moment.

Lorenzo laid eyes upon them and knew they were Kataryna's children. They looked just like how Raven had described the princess to Gezana. The older two had her black eyes, the younger one, however, he could not believe his own eyes. Looking back at him were Raven's eyes, but how could that be? Could the Fates have intervened? He took a step toward Amara. "Your eyes, they…"

She looked almost sheepish, "I know…I have her eyes. It is a sign that it was meant to be, that the Fates want them together. Now we must help them to believe in it as well."

✝

Lorenzo escorted them below deck. "Please be cautious, she is very upset." As he opened the door, they overheard Gezana telling Raven to stop acting like a petulant child.

They watched as she pulled her sword on Gezana. This woman standing before them wielding her sword was not the same woman they met just that morning. Amara watched as Raven's aura turned darker and darker, further losing the remainder of herself as it did. As she watched, Amara felt an evil take over Raven. She feared what would happen if she did not put a stop to it.

Raven pushed the tip of the sword into his neck, causing Gezana to wince. Her body was tightly wound, ready for battle. "You knew! You knew! Why?"

Amara pushed by her siblings and stepped into the room. She put herself in between Raven and Gezana. "No more bloodshed! No more! The time is past for recriminations. We must let go of the past. All have done things that are regrettable. We must forgive and go forward. Let us sit and you will tell us of how you and our mother met instead."

There was something about Amara that commanded attention, even Raven was taken aback at the forcefulness the young girl possessed.

Raven gazed into Amara's eyes. It was like looking in a mirror. She laid her sword on the table without even knowing she was doing so. "Your eyes, they are mine. How…how is that possible?" She shook her head, feeling the anger leave her body. "It matters not at this time."

Raven waved the others into the room. Something in Amara called to her. She made the decision to trust her.

"Sometimes others know best. Please sit all of you. I have a story to tell."

Lorenzo slipped away and returned a short time later with food. Raven was well into the tale, but that did not worry him, he knew Gezana would fill him in later.

Upon conclusion of Raven's tale, the three told their tale. It was a tale of a princess who became Queen and was made into the Dragon. By the end, Raven sat with head in her hands. What had become of her princess? Had this been her fault? Had she caused Kat to turn into the Dragon?

Raven felt more defeated than ever. "It...it is my fault this has happened and I have not a clue on how to make it right. I do not think I ever could make this right, no matter what I do. Thank you for coming here." She retreated to her cabin, where she sobbed in solitude.

†

Knowing what they must do, Bryanne, Aiden, and Amara returned to the palace. They went to convince their mother to see Raven once more. Upon their arrival, they retold the story of who the betrayer truly was. The three sat at the long table in the war room as Kataryna paced the length from one end to the other.

Kataryna stopped dead in her tracks, the gravity of the situation finally hitting her. "Even in death the bastard still betrays me. All I have done, all that I am, was based on a lie. Death was too good for him! He deserves an eternity of torture." She turned one last time and looked at her children.

"I...I will go see her, although I cannot guarantee she will listen to me."

✝

Amara followed her mother to the stables. "Please, Mother, let one of us go with you. Your presence may not be looked upon as favorable."

The Dragon mounted her horse, pulled on the reins and started out of the stables. Calling over her shoulder she replied, "No, this I must do on my own."

✝

Unknown to the Dragon, all three of her children followed her. They could not let her go alone, it was their duty to watch over her and feeling it was their burden to bear if this did not end well. As they traveled, the twins became aware that even Amara was worried. Her always apparent smile was lost. Replaced by a frown, which in turn terrified Bryanne and Aiden more than anything ever had.

Kataryna rode swiftly through the streets toward the docks, not knowing what she would say upon arrival. Something was driving her toward Raven but she knew not what. It was only that she had to see her once more.

Upon arrival at the docks, Kat knew by instinct which ship was Raven's. She found the crew and ship preparing for departure. Kat thought of not seeing Raven one last time and her heart stopped. Could she have been wrong all these years? Did Raven truly love her and she love Raven in return?

As she dismounted her horse, she once again cursed Renaldo for denying her Raven's love. "Do not worry, Renaldo, we will meet again one day and I will make you pay for what you have done." She quietly vowed to herself.

Kat stood on the dock watching Raven move about the deck, giving commands to her crew.

It was not the Dragon that walked up the gangplank onto the ship, but Kataryna. She stepped onto the ship and waited for Raven to notice her presence.

Gezana had seen her the moment she rode up but did not inform Raven. This was something she needed to do on her own.

†

Ordering her crew to make ready, Raven heard the horse gallop up but never gave it another thought. Raven felt as if she were being studied, yet knew it was none of her own crew. Now she felt watched. She slowly turned and laid eyes upon the intruder. Involuntarily her body took a step back, as if being slapped by an invisible hand. She was here, upon her ship. What did she want? Did she want her head in a pirate's noose? Raven stood defiant against her.

"We are preparing to leave as you requested, Dragon. Do you wish for us to leave faster?" She moved her hand to the hilt of her sword, preparing for a fight. Her crew ceased all motion, unsure what was happening.

†

Kataryna held her hands up away from her sword. Something had changed inside of her and she wanted no fight this day. Not with this woman. Her eyes traveled up Raven's body and set upon her face.

For the first time in many, many seasons, Kat felt a peace come over her. How could this woman affect her so? "I...I came to tell you, you may stay if you wish."

Raven's heart skipped a beat. Was she hearing her correctly? What she was not hearing was Kataryna asking her to stay only that she 'was allowed to stay.' Raven wanted her to want her to stay. One thing was for sure, before her stood Kataryna not the Dragon.

"What do you, Kataryna, want?" Raven folded her hands behind her back and waited. "Do you want me to stay?"

Standing before her was not the Raven she remembered, yet it was. She was now more powerful, more defiant. Kataryna's stubbornness ruled over her. "Do as you wish. Stay or leave, it makes no matter, it is too late to change things. They are what they are."

Raven studied her. What she saw tore at her heart. Her princess seemed so utterly defeated. She knew it might be her undoing but she spoke from the heart. "This is not who you are. You are not this Dragon. There is love and passion somewhere inside of you. They are hidden and need to find their way out. More so than anything, you have honor inside of you. I have seen it. I know it is there." She held her hands out to Kataryna, as if pleading with her. "Is that why you banished your father?" Raven took a step toward her. "You did not want him to see what you were becoming." Another step... And yet another... "You knew he was ashamed," now within arm's length, "he would not have wanted to see his grandchildren becoming warlords."

Kataryna stood transfixed. Raven did know her heart, her very soul. However, once again stubbornness ruled. "How dare you!"

151

Across the deck walked Bryanne, with her sword drawn. She had heard enough. "Enough! I have had enough!" Bryanne stood in front of her mother and faced her. She bent and placed her sword at Kataryna's feet. "It is over mother. I can no longer condone this. We have gone against our people for too long. It is time for us to stand with them. To fight...for them..." She strode over to Raven and bowed to her. She then turned to face her mother once more as she now stood by Raven's side.

Aiden then followed suit. He added his bow and short sword to his sister's sword at their mother's feet. He also then bowed to Raven and came to take up position on her left side.

Kataryna was speechless. She watched as Amara came to stand by her. She looked up at her mother, then at Raven. "Welcome home, both of you." Amara then turned and left the ship.

†

Unsure what to do, Raven stopped her crew from making ready the ship to leave. She needed time to think. She needed solitude. Raven retreated to her quarters to contemplate what had taken place. Could she stay? She was not sure. On the other hand, could she leave?

Long after the moon had risen high in the night sky, Raven stood on deck looking out over the bay. The rest of the crew long asleep in their bunks, she kept sentry over the ship. From behind, she heard a board creak. "Why are you up, Gez? Go back to bed. I am sure Lorenzo is missing you." She turned and rested her back against the railing.

152

"You know I will not go, so do not ask again. What troubles you? Tell me your thoughts." He leaned by her side facing the other direction, toward the water.

"Should I?" The question sounded weak, yet she did not care.

"That is for you alone to decide, my friend. Do not let your past rule your future. You must do what is in your soul. You are special. The Fates have given you a second chance. What do you want? What do you need inside of you?" He turned toward her, leaning his hip against the weathered wood.

Raven closed her eyes while contemplating his words. She searched deep inside of herself for the answer. The waters surrounding them grew still. Clouds engulfed the moon, plunging further darkness over the night. It was as if Raven's emotions ruled the elements.

Opening her eyes, she faced her friend. Tears flowed. The pain etched on her face. "What I need is for these past seasons to never have happened. I need her love as I need the air that I breathe. I need my Kataryna back. That is what I need, yet will never have. I can never go back to what should have been. I have to look at what I have at this moment in time."

He put one hand on her shoulder and wiped at the tears with the other. Under normal conditions she would have killed any man that touched her, this however, was far from the normal. "Shall we stay a sunrise or two then? Maybe see what the next one brings."

"Yes, let us do that. Now go back to your cabin. I am sure he is pacing by now."

Gezana bowed. "Yes ma'am." He took a few steps across the deck.

153

"Gez...thanks. I would surely be lost if not for you." She turned and gazed out over the water once more.

At sunrise, she informed the crew they were staying for at least the next sunrise. She, however, wanted them to be ready to leave at a moment's notice. She had Lorenzo send several crewmen into town to barter for what supplies they could find. Others she told to go to the tavern and have a good evening, leaving only a skeleton crew aboard to continue preparations.

Raven remained in her quarters, lying upon her bed studying the blue diamond she held in her hand. Her hair free from its braid, covered her pillow. She felt more relaxed than she had in a long time.

Lorenzo knocked and entered upon approval from Raven. He sat her evening meal on her desk.

She once again held the gem up to the firelight. "'Tis it not beautiful, unlike anything you have ever seen?"

He stepped over and set eyes upon the diamond. "It is quite unique."

She dropped it back into the blue velvet pouch she kept it in for safekeeping. "I bought it what seems like a lifetime ago. Now I...well I..." She could not put into words what she felt. She was too confused.

Lorenzo took a chance. "You thought it a nice wedding ring for your princess."

Her head snapped up. A shy grin appeared on her face. "Am I so transparent?"

Lorenzo knew to choose his words carefully. "Only those very few who know you well are able to see when you think of her. You wear your soul upon your chest. This is not a bad thing, not when the time is right. Use these feelings to help in your decisions. Let the love you still feel tell you what to do. I must now take Gez his meal, he is preparing the charts in the strategy room."

A heartbeat after her door closed, a deafening sound filled the air. Bolting up from her chair, she was through the door without another thought, grabbing her sword as she went. Raven knew that sound. It was not a good sound. Anytime she heard it and it was not her own, it sent chills through her. Passing the strategy room, she threw open the door. "Cannon fire!" She continued running, up the stairs to the deck. "All hands...DEFEND!"

She found Lorenzo already on deck with his sword in his hand. "Get to the palace! Warn the queen. Then pick up the rest of the crew from the tavern on your way back. We will hold them off as long as we can until reinforcements get here. Now go!"

With Gezana by her side, they met the pirates head on. In what seemed like only heartbeats later Bryanne, Aiden, and the palace troops were fighting for their very lives. They fought side by side with Raven and her crew.

Raven deflected an arrow meant for Gezana's chest. She looked around to see where it came from. She turned to her left toward town and saw nothing. As she spun around toward the dock once more, she saw a silhouette of a figure on the end of the pier release an arrow. Its direction suddenly came to her. There was no humanly possible way for her to intercept it before it hit its target.

The scream that ripped from Raven's chest was unlike anything any had ever heard. It was not human. It sounded of a giant beast of an animal was wounded and dying. She reached her target in time to catch her body as it fell. The arrow had found its home.

Bryanne felt the last breath leave her body as she landed in Raven's arms. She looked up at the older woman, wishing she had somehow had the time to get to know her. To know the woman her mother had loved. That she still loved.

Raven felt Gezana standing next to her holding two pirates off at once. She looked down at the lifeless body in her arms. The last thread of her sanity snapped. Raven let loose the beast she'd kept contained over the last several seasons. She gently laid Bryanne down onto the cold ground, smoothing Bryanne's damp hair from her face.

Slowly she stood, picking up her sword, never talking her eyes from her soul's daughter. The very air surrounding her crackled with fire as death descended upon them. Her blood boiled in her veins. A look came over her face none had ever seen. A sudden swift wind came in from the bay. It seemed to swirl only around Raven. As it did, her long black hair flowed freely, causing her to look like her given name, El Diablo.

Gezana did not know the woman who now stood beside him. Never in all the seasons he had fought beside her had he seen such a dead look in her eyes; such an evil look, as if all humanity had left her. It was not Raven who stood beside him, but the beast that only Hades himself could contain.

It was not Bryanne that Raven saw lying on the ground, but Kataryna's lifeless body. Picking up Bryanne's sword she turned to face their attackers with a sword in each hand. "BASTARDS! I will see you all in Hades!" She was obsessed as she slashed her way through the pirates.

As heads rolled from bodies, her own crew moved out of her way in fear she would kill them as well, knowing she could no longer tell one from the other. All she saw was crimson blood before her eyes.

As one pirate after another fell, Aiden watched Raven as he made his way to his sister. He had known the moment his twin took her last breath for he also felt his own heart stop. Something inside him died as she died. He then watched the transformation come over Raven. Fighting off one last man, Aiden knelt beside Bryanne. He wept for his sister's lost life.

Turning, Raven saw a man kneeling beside her love's lifeless body. "NO! Do not dare touch her! You will die for touching my princess!" She lunged toward Aiden, unable to grasp the reality of whom it was or where she was.

Gezana grabbed Raven from behind around the waist and held fast to her. Two others from her crew each grabbed an arm and held on as if their lives depended on it. Lorenzo called to her trying to break through the barriers. "Raven...Raven, it is Lorenzo. Look at me...It is not Kataryna. Do you understand? It is not her."

Raven continued to fight as if she were a caged animal trying to free herself. "No! You lie!"

Aiden stood and faced her. "Raven...look at me. It is Aiden. It is not my mother. It is Bryanne. Please look and see with your soul's eyes who it is."

She gazed down at the body and gasped. It was not Kataryna, but Bryanne who lay upon the ground. "By the Gods..." They let go of her and she dropped to her knees beside her.

"I was not in time. Not in time...I should have been in time. It should have been me not her. I should be lying here instead." She pulled the arrow out, picked Bryanne up and started to walk to the palace.

The remaining pirates on shore were rounded up, in preparation for transportation to the palace dungeons. The ship they arrived in was already under way leaving the others behind.

Gezana stepped forward as if to take Bryanne from her arms. "No! I must do this. I must be the one."

With Gezana, Lorenzo, and Aiden following behind her, she walked the entire way to the palace carrying Bryanne's body in her arms. Never once did she feel the lifeless weight, instead it felt as if she carried a small bundle of clothes.

As Raven walked through the palace gate the aura that rolled off her warned all not to touch her. She made her way up the steps and into the great hall. There her eyes rose and met another's.

A great wail was heard through the palace as Kataryna took Bryanne's body from Raven. For a moment, Raven saw Kataryna standing in front of her.

"Hang the ones who did this! I want them dead! Every last one of them!" She turned and laid her daughter on the banquet table. She then turned back to Raven.

"You?! Why did you not keep her safe? Why did you not take the death that came for her? Why?" The grief that washed over her was then replaced with anger. Anger directed at Raven herself. Drawing her sword, she advanced on Raven.

Raven realized almost too late, the Dragon was back in place. Kataryna was gone, perhaps forever. Her crew moved to stand between them. Raven held out her arms to stop them, conveying in her unspoken words to stand down.

Raven would not fight her. If the Dragon wished to kill her, so be it. That would be her destiny. They stood boot to boot, each looking into the other's eyes. They stood looking for something, neither not knowing what.

Dragon pulled her short sword and pressed it against Raven's throat. Raven did not flinch. She did not so much as twitch a muscle. The Dragon's hand shook with the fury inside of her. She pressed the blade into Raven's throat and she watched as a trickle of blood ran down Raven's neck.

"Get on your ship and leave now or I will finish what this blade has started. Her death is on your head. Never forget this moment when you look back." She turned, picked up her daughter's lifeless body and left the great hall.

Lorenzo ripped a piece of his shirt off and slipped it into Gezana's hand, who then pressed it to Raven's neck. She pushed his hand away, not wanting the sympathy. Raven turned on her heels and left, without looking back.

As she raced back to her ship, Raven barked out orders to her crew. They were making ready to set sail immediately. "I want this ship ready to set sail at first light! Now move, all of you."

She stood on deck gazing in the direction of the palace. Gezana stepped up and took his place beside her. He felt nothing but sorrow at the events that had taken place. "There is nothing you could have done. It was her destiny to die this day. You are not at fault. No one was at fault but the one who shot the arrow."

There were no tears now, all been previously shed. Now, there was only regret at what could have been. Raven resigned herself to the reality that all was lost. "We have arrived too late, my old friend. My princess, my soul, my life has been gone a very long time. I am weary of this life, let us go home, old friend."

Chapter Nine

"Are we ready? It is almost sunrise and I told you I wanted to be gone before this." Raven turned toward her crew. She knew she was pushing them but did not care. Several of them were injured and all of them were bone tired. Yet Raven worked them as if they were slaves, barking out orders to them as she walked the planks.

Raven wanted gone from the place that held nothing but anger and remorse for her. She wanted to be at sea, where she could be free. The crew seemed to be moving too slow for Raven's liking. "If anyone of you cannot handle your duties, you will be replaced! Of course, though, I am sure none of you would like the reason you would be replaced. You have had all night to prepare. NOW MOVE! I want to get away from here as fast as possible."

†

Gezana had never seen her so angry. He knew her anger was not at the crew but at herself. A few moments before, Lorenzo had been on the receiving end of her temper when he brought her morning meal.

Lorenzo had knocked and gone into her room upon her barking, "Enter!" He set the tray upon the table. She looked at the food thinking to herself that Bryanne could no longer enjoy even the simple pleasures in life. Raven blamed herself the young woman's death and no one could tell her otherwise.

Seeing the look in her eyes Lorenzo started to walk backward toward the door. He did not make it out before she picked up the tray and threw it in his direction. He had to duck to avoid being hit; the tray hitting the door behind him.

"When I want something to eat I will ask for it! Now clean up that mess and leave me alone!" She pushed him out of the way, flung the door open, and stormed out.

Raven could not stop herself as the anger coursed through her.

✝

Gezana stepped up beside her, saying nothing, waiting for her to speak. She stood leaning over the railing. When she looked up at him her eyes were not her own, gone were the beautiful crystal-blue eyes that had always looked back at him. The eyes that looked back at him disturbed him deeply, however he could not look away.

"Yes, you wanted something?" She heard the venom in her voice and it startled her. She could not control it. The beast had taken control. There was nothing left of her former self.

Gezana stood transfixed, looking into her eyes that now held no color; the blue had become crystal clear. What he saw in them was pure evil. This was not the woman he

161

had fought side by side with over the past fifteen seasons, nor was she the woman that had become his friend. He prayed to whatever god would listen that she would return to him.

He wanted to draw out from her the battle that was going on inside of her, but he knew he did not dare. He would wait until they arrived home. He did not want to lose his head, so he chose to wait. "We are ready to leave."

It was then they heard the commotion on the dock. When Gezana looked, he was not shocked by who it was. He knew they would show sooner or later.

When Raven saw them, she stopped short. She had not expected them to come. She assumed they, too, would blame her for their sister's death.

Gezana shouted to the crew standing guard on the dock. "Leave them be. Do not touch them."

Amara and Aiden had approached the ship warily not knowing how they would be received. The crew had descended upon them in a rush. Aiden drew his short sword in order to defend them. When he heard Gezana's voice, he was relieved.

Aiden's relief was short-lived as one of the crew that the pirates had picked up only a few short moons ago either did not hear Gezana or paid no attention to him. He advanced on Amara, grabbing her around the waist as he tried to kiss her. With that action his fate was sealed.

Raven vaulted over the railing of the ship, landing on the deck, shocking all of them. She took the offender by the neck, causing him to release Amara and lifted him from the ground. She growled at him as she pulled her sword and ran him through with it. She then tossed his lifeless body to the ground.

Looking each of her crew in the eyes, she dared any one of them to protest. All returned to their duties but for Gezana, who stood beside her. Two of them took the body away. She then turned to Amara. "I am sorry, *my lady,* for such behavior. Sometimes my men get a little out of hand. What may I do for you?"

The siblings then saw her eyes. Aiden visibly shuddered. Amara cried out. They saw deadness reflected back at them. The woman who was to become their mother's savior was no more. In her place, a demon had sprouted.

Amara knew that many seasons ago, the Gods gave her mother, Kataryna, a gift. Of this Amara was now positive. When she first laid eyes upon Raven, she had known what that gift was. It was that Raven was her true mother by blood and Amara had been the gift to Kat; the gift of a child from her soul mate.

Amara spoke without thought from her heart to the woman she now knew was her mother as well. "Please, Mother, do not blame yourself. It was your destiny to leave when you did. There was nothing anyone could have done to stop it from happening."

Upon hearing Amara call her 'Mother,' Raven dropped her sword as shock washed over. She could not deny the reality of it. The young woman standing before her was indeed herself. How could this be though? How could she be Amara's mother? "How...I..."

Amara laid her hand upon Raven's face, cradling her cheek in the palm of her left hand. Surprised when Raven did not flinch or move away, she spoke. "The Gods do things we do not understand, for reasons we will never know. Know this though. You are not to blame for any of it."

Raven leaned into the touch. "I...I should never have left."

Amara felt a small spark of humanity return to Raven. Seeing that spark she knew what she had to do; she had to push further. It was the only way to get her to return to them. "You had to leave. You were destined to leave, just as it is now destiny that you were to return. Do you think it is by chance that you are here now? The Fates have brought you to us. I implore you to listen to them." Amara laid her head upon her mother's chest. For the first time in her life, the young girl felt complete peace.

Raven slid her arms around her and held her. She set her chin upon Amara's head. "My daughter...our daughter..."

Amara looked up at her as a single tear slid down Raven's cheek. She looked into her eyes and saw the glacier that had become her eyes did not change. Amara knew in that instant that she would not be able to change Raven's mind to make her stay. She had failed, a piece of her heart tore off and floated away.

"I am afraid I cannot, child. Too much has happened. My princess is dead and gone and I have followed her. It was she that I love, that I would die for. Both of us took the wrong paths many seasons ago. I am truly sorry." Raven stepped back from Amara.

Aiden had heard enough. In his heart, he thought he could bring her back to them. "Enough! You are not to blame for any of this. If you truly loved our mother, you will stay. You are a coward if you leave."

All watched as Raven's body tensed as if ready to strike. The beast was completely back in place once more. Gezana stepped forward. "Boy..." Raven stopped him with a hand pressed to his chest.

Raven took a defensive step toward Aiden. "Listen to me very closely, little boy. It is because you are her son that you are not now dead. Do not dare cross my path again, because the next time I will not be so kind." Her voice, body, and mannerisms no longer held a shred of humanity. She turned to Amara.

"Mother, I..." Amara stopped. No words would bring Raven back to them.

A growl came from deep within her; from the hollowness where her soul and heart had once been. "I am no one's mother. It is best to remember that, little one. What I am is sure death and destruction. *I am El Diablo.*" She turned, leaving behind only the echo of her boots on the wooden planks.

Gezana watched her leave and turned back to the children of his captain's long-lost love. "I am sorry."

Amara picked up Raven's sword, studied it a moment and then handed it to him. "Watch over her. The worst is yet to come." Then she too turned and walked away with Aiden following close behind her.

†

As they entered their mother's chambers, where she had secluded herself, Kataryna saw the utter defeat upon their faces. Neither of them had told her where they were going, yet she had known. She knew they would try to convince Raven to stay, just as she knew what the outcome would be.

Kataryna's emotions were in turmoil, the last several sunsets had sent her mind spinning. She was angered to see Raven, yet happy beyond words. Her anger then soared when she found out Renaldo had further betrayed her. Overshadowing that was the love she still felt deep in her soul for Raven. But it all came crashing down around her

165

when Raven walked in carrying her dead daughter in her arms.

She knew what they had come to tell her, it was written upon their faces. "Yes...?"

Amara stepped forward. It would be best coming from her, not Aiden. "Raven is setting sail."

"I know. I knew she would leave. Why should she stay? I am not whom she was looking for. I had no faith that she would stay." They heard the hollowness in their mother's voice.

"Mother..." Kataryna held up her hand to stop Amara from saying more.

"No. I knew what would happen once she saw who the Dragon was. I am ashamed of who I have become, of what I have become. Raven was correct in leaving here and never looking back. She is right to leave me now in my misery, having nothing to do with me." She sighed and stood from her chair. "She is also correct that Father would be and is ashamed of me. Aiden, I have a mission for you, a very special mission. I want you to bring your grandfather home." She saw the shock on their faces.

"Mother, I do not know..." Aiden stopped when Kataryna glared in his direction.

"I know you have visited with him, so do not finish that sentence. You will go and bring him home after we bury Bryanne at sunset. Amara, we have many things to change in this palace. It is time I ruled, as he would have wanted me to. We need to meet with the lords and find someone to take on the responsibilities for the guards." Plans were spinning in her head on how she would win her people back.

Amara did not move from where she stood as Kataryna started for the door, expecting her daughter to follow. "Well, are you coming?"

"Mother, there is something I must tell you...about Grandfather."

Kataryna stopped and turned back toward them.

"I had him brought home several moons ago. He is staying in the old temple outside the palace. I will go and bring him home. Back where he belongs."

Kataryna could not believe her ears. How did Amara know? Her daughter was a constant and utter mystery to her. For the first time in her life, she looked at her daughter and did not fear her. She looked at her with love in her eyes. It was in that moment in time she came to realize Amara was her daughter, yet she was not. Somehow, someway she had given birth those years ago to Raven's daughter.

"By the Gods...you are Raven's daughter, are you not? I do not understand how, but I know it to be true. Just as I do not know how you knew she was coming."

"Yes Mother, I am. What is more important is I am the daughter of both of you. Even though I was not born first, I was born out of love. I was made from the love you have for her and with her." Amara tilted her head to one side as if listening to something only she could hear.

Her expression saddened. "Do not worry, Mother, you will see her again soon." Amara walked by her brother and Kataryna, then out the door to finalize preparations for King Theos's return.

"Aiden send messengers to all the lords that the Dragon is gone and Queen Kataryna now rules in her place, but remind them this palace still rules over all the lands. I will be in the war room, preparing for the battles to come." She smiled at him, for the first time in many seasons.

As the sun set and the moon rose all those who resided in the palace gathered at the crypt on the hill that overlooked the valley below. Bryanne was laid to rest next to

167

her grandmother as Kataryna stood silently by, watching all around her.

She wondered what they thought. Did they blame her for her daughter's death? She was sure they did. Kataryna blamed herself. The priest prayed as they sealed the stone with Bryanne's name upon it.

Returning to the palace, Kataryna retired to her chambers to mourn in private. Being the queen, she could not show weakness by grieving in public. She knew over the next several moons there would be changes within the palace walls and she welcomed them. Several of the lords would not like the changes and would rebel. The following morning she planned to meet with Aiden and her new commander of the palace guards and decide on what action to take should any of the lords attack.

†

Several sunrises later found many changes in the castle as well as on the seas. Kataryna made her plans to defend her lands as Raven and her crew fought for their very lives.

†

Raven spent the morning in her cabin, just as she had every other moment since leaving port. She refused most meals Lorenzo brought her. She sat deep in thought, contemplating how horribly wrong things had gone. Raven thought of how she had loved Kat and how that love, had brought her nothing but heartache.

168

It was then that she heard shouting and men running. Lorenzo threw open her cabin door and stopped. He tried t catch his breath as he spoke. "Ship, attacking...colors...Lenara..." He flew from the room after delivering his message.

"Damn her! She said we could leave. Damn her to Hades!" Raven grabbed her sword as she ran from the room in preparation to fight.

Arriving on deck, she found her ship being boarded by the Lenara soldiers. Her eyes landed upon Gezana. "How..." She needed not ask the full question.

"We saw them approaching and thought they would pass us by. We assumed they had received word we were not to be touched." Gezana fought off one of the first soldiers that set foot on the ship. She looked around seeing that her men had not even had time to load the cannons, just as she also realized they were gravely outnumbered.

Raven shouted to the soldiers as they boarded her ship. "I am the captain of this ship and I have been granted pardon by the ruler of these waters." The soldiers ignored her pleas.

Two soldiers came after her. She fought them off, killing one of them as she saw one of her own men go down. She then watched as another two of her men fell to the deck lifeless. "NO! Damn you...the Dragon told us we would be unharmed... Leave my ship!"

†

Moments before as Gezana fought his attacker, the commander of *The Liberty* stood waiting for Raven to turn and fight him. She finally dispatched the man she was fighting and turned to him.

He smiled. "At last, I finally meet the famous female pirate. I am sure you will hang and die the same as any other pirate."

"Why do you fight us? The Dragon promised us no harm would come to us if we left her port." Raven spread her legs a little wider and raised her two swords in preparation to fight.

"I received no such instructions." He leered at her thinking of the fun he would have with her before she would die. He would make her beg to die. "Surrender now, I have no wish to see you dead, yet."

A laugh with no humor in it erupted from Raven. "Forget it, little man, you will never touch me like you want to. I would die before I let you, as would all my crew before they let you touch me."

In hearing her words, her remaining crew fought twice as hard. As their swords clashed, the two leaders circled each other. Each looked for the other's weaknesses. Raven was the first to act. She lunged at the commander, grazing his arm. He had not expected her to go on the offense and was caught off guard. This, however, was the only time.

Raven laughed maniacally. "Yes, little man, today is a good day to die! Whether it be you, or if the Fates finally allow it, me." Raven lunged again, finding he matched her blow for blow.

After a few moments of fighting the commander, Raven watched helpless as Gezana fell to the deck from a blow to the head, just as she felt excruciating pain in her shoulder. She looked down to find a sword had been run through her shoulder.

Raven had not sensed the man behind her in time due to being distracted, by the falling of her friend. "Your men have no honor if they attack from behind, Commander." As the sword was pulled from her shoulder, she turned her attention back to the man in front of her as she felt his sword slice through her side. Had she not turned when she did, it would have landed through her belly instead.

Raven's mind reeled, how had she lost? How had this come to be? How would she protect her crew? Her knees buckled and she landed on them in front of the commander. She looked from the sword being pulled from her body to the man standing over her.

She spoke the first words to come to her. "We surrender, take us to Pavlone." She then collapsed lifeless to the deck, inches from her friend. Her last thought was of her beloved Kataryna. "Kat...my love..."

✝

Sometime later Gezana woke to find Lorenzo, three others, and himself the only remaining crew alive, locked in cells below the enemy's deck. Lying on the cot in the next cell was Raven's lifeless form. "NO! It cannot be! It is not to end like this! It cannot!"

Gezana tried the cell door and found it locked. He knew it would be but he tried anyway. "Guard! Guard!" He shook the door and Lorenzo tried to quiet him.

"Shh...please do not call them. There is nothing we can do for her now. We must keep ourselves alive so we may tell the queen what has happened. Please, quiet down." He tried to pull Gezana from the door.

"NO! She cannot be dead. If she is dead, all is lost. All will be lost!" He sat on the floor and sobbed.

As Gezana sobbed, a guard approached the cell. Lorenzo knew this man. It had been so long since he had laid eyes upon him. The guard standing in front of him was his brother, Baylor. "Baylor, please…is she…" Lorenzo could not even form the words.

Many seasons had passed since last he had seen his little brother. Baylor would know him anywhere. And he could not harm him even knowing he was a pirate.

Without any words, Baylor opened the cell to where Lorenzo and Gezana were and then the one to where Raven laid. Baylor then turned and walked away. Gezana was through the open door and at Raven's bedside in less than a heartbeat.

Gezana knelt beside her and laid his fingers upon her neck. There was a faint pulse. "She lives. Lorenzo, she is alive!"

Lorenzo rushed into the cell, ripping his shirt from his back. He tore it into strips and began to care for Raven's wounds. "She needs a healer, if she is to live. We should be in port anytime, let us hope they send for one once they find out their error."

†

Find out their error they did. Upon docking, they informed the dockmaster they had pirate prisoners from a ship that had just sailed from that very dock several sunrises before. The commander also informed them they had the female captain as his prisoner.

The dockmaster shrank back in fear. He knew what the penalty would be for harming her and her crew. "Commander, I fear I have grave news. Captain Raven and her crew left these waters under the protection of the Dragon. Please…tell me you have not harmed any of them, have you?"

The commander was shocked and dismayed as he turned to see his prisoners carrying the pirate captain's body from the cells below. Raven's remaining crewmembers were shackled, which made the task of being careful even more difficult.

The dockmaster yelled to one of his underlings to fetch a healer and meet them at the inn. He knew someone would pay with his life for this and he did not want it to be him. He would do everything possible to save her life.

†

Kataryna hesitated outside her father's chambers. He had returned home to the palace two sunrises before, but she did not have the courage until that moment to face him. She came to him seeking his forgiveness. She knocked, entering when she heard his gravelly voice. Kat meekly looked about the room. It was the first time since she had banished him that she had set foot in his rooms. After sending him away, she had them locked and permitted no one to enter them.

She found him seated in his wingback leather chair in front of the fire. Kataryna knelt in front of him. Upon looking up at him, she broke down and sobbed. Laying her head upon his knee, he raised his hand and stroked her head. "Father, it is good to have you home. I have made so many mistakes. Please forgive me for what I have done and for what I have become. I have lost one of my children because of my ignorance. Oh, Father, what am I to do? I have driven her away…the only person to ever matter."

King Theos knew of what his daughter had become, just as he knew of every despicable injustice she had carelessly flung upon her people. Still he was her father and

173

he loved her. They would get through this, ruling the lands as had all generations before them.

"My daughter, all is not lost. All can be undone with forgiveness. I have never stopped loving you, as your people have never stopped. They await your return as their queen. I am sorry for the loss of Bryanne. I would have liked to have known her, as I have known Amara and Aiden. You have raised wonderful children who love you, their mother, very much; children who would do anything you ask." He rose and crossed the room to his desk.

Her eyes followed him, thinking how very wrong he was. She had done too many despicable things to ever be forgiven. How could anyone forgive her, if she could not forgive herself? Kataryna blamed herself for everything that had happened.

He pulled from the desk a velvet pouch. "These were your mother's and mine, they are now yours. Go after her, if you truly love her." Unaware of Kataryna's inner turmoil he emptied the contents into her hand.

There in her palm lay the two most beautiful rings she had ever seen. They were gold bands with small sapphires set in between small diamonds on half of each ring. She instinctively knew they would fit her and Raven's fingers, just as they had her parents. Kataryna did not feel worthy of such a gift. The weight of all the misery she felt crashed down upon her once more. Self-hatred coursed through showing itself in her defeated body. "No, it was not meant to be. It is too late, Father. She hates me and has left." She handed the rings back to her father. "Keep them for Aiden one day." She turned and left his chamber.

✝

A messenger from the docks arrived at the palace as Kataryna made her way back to her chambers. She did not care what had happened at the port. She waved him away and told him to tell Amara what they needed. He informed her that it was not her, but Amara that he sought. Upon hearing that, Kataryna continued on to her chambers.

Amara knew something grave had happened. She ran through the hallway to the main entrance, with her skirts billowing behind her. She skidded to a halt in front of the young man who had been speaking with her mother. She knew in her heart what he was there to tell her. Amara called for one of the guards.

"Yes, Princess, how can I be of service?" He stood at attention, awaiting her commands.

"Find my brother. Tell him to meet me at the inn. Tell him it is urgent, it is a matter of life or death. Now hurry!" She turned to the young man and studied him for a moment. "Come, we must hurry. There is no time to waste."

Amara arrived at the inn where she was taken to a back room. She entered to find the room lit by a single candle. An overwhelming feeling of death hung in the room. Even with that feeling, she knew in her heart Raven was not dead yet. If she had been, Amara would have known. She would have felt it in her soul.

She knelt beside the bed and quickly prayed for guidance from the Goddesses. Amara then set about her task of cleaning the wounds in preparation for healing her. She vaguely heard her brother enter the room and gasp. Without looking up, she gave him a mission. "Aiden, you must go get Mother, tell her what has happened. You must hurry. However, you must prepare her for what she will see."

Aiden hesitated and then rushed from the room. Making his way through the inn, he came face-to-face with

175

the man who had disobeyed his mother's wishes. When he returned he would deal with him. "Stay here and make sure Amara has everything she needs. If Raven dies, so will you. The only difference being you will die a long and painful death."

The commander bowed his head. "Yes my Prince, as you wish."

✝

Aiden moved swiftly to the palace to inform their mother as Amara started to heal Raven the best she could. She could help to heal her bodily wounds. However, there was nothing she could do for her soul.

Amara cleaned the wounds of dirt and infection. She then poured her healing solution into them. Satisfied they were cleaned as best as she could do, she set about stitching them. She did not want to cauterize them, wanting any infection that she missed coming out instead of remaining in the wound.

Raven only stirred once throughout the ordeal. Amara thought it a miracle that she still lived. She knew it was not Raven's time to meet Hades. Not yet. "Oh Mother, please come back to us, we need you. Mama needs you."

✝

As Aiden raced through town to the palace grounds, two races of another sort had started at the inn, one to save a life and the other to save one's own skin from being stripped from its bones.

Amara would need every ounce of knowledge known to her to save Raven. She called deep within herself for the strength she would need. The establishment owner and others feared to go in the room; they feared to even be in the building.

Not one of them wanted to be caught in the backlash that was sure to come once the Dragon knew what had happened. The commander had sent for Baylor, his second in command. He knew of only one way to save his own skin; sacrifice that of another.

Knowing no one would hear her Amara spoke aloud. "I can do this. I have to do this. She cannot die." She smoothed the sweat- and blood-laden hair back from Raven's face. She continued to stir the mixture into the tea that would hopefully reduce Raven's fever. The next trick would be to get the tea down her throat.

The mixture now done, only the next step eluded her. "Please Fates, I know you watch over her, you must now help her. Give her the strength to return to us. She must return to us, she is our only hope." She looked down at Raven. "May the Gods give me strength, I must get you to drink this, yet I do not know how."

The door opened behind Amara. "Let me try." Kataryna quietly closed the door. She turned, gasping when she saw the body spread out before her. Her hand instinctively went to her sword. Thoughts raged through Kat's mind of how the commander would pay with his life for doing this. Closing her eyes, she steeled her nerve. Now was not the time for those thoughts. Raven needed her. She would deal with him later.

✝

Amara's smile extended from ear to ear. This was the next step of many for a new beginning that Kataryna would make. Amara stood so that Kataryna could sit on the side of the bed.

The queen removed her sword, setting it on the floor beside the bed. Once more, she thought of the ones responsible and the anger in her welled anew. Kataryna sat looking down at the broken and battered body of the woman she loved more than life itself. In that moment, she knew that if Raven died so would she, but not before those responsible were dealt a horrific death.

Laying her hand upon Raven's cheek, Kat felt the fever that raged in her body. Kataryna gently lifted her and slid herself behind her pirate, so that she could cradle her body against her own. She laid Raven's head upon her chest and took the cup from Amara's hand. Kataryna once again laid her hand upon Raven's cheek. She stroked the skin, trying to will life to return to it. "Darling, I need you to wake up, just for a moment. I need you to drink this for me."

No response…no life stirred within her body.

Tears streamed down Kataryna's face. She set the cup upon the table and pulled her tighter against her body. The heat pouring from Raven's body sank into her own and renewed her effort. "Raven, my love, I want you to wake up right now. We need you…I need you. Please…" Still there was no response.

She put her lips to Raven's ear. "I love you, I always have. I need you. I cannot live this life any longer without you. You are my soul, my life, my every breath. Now open those amazing eyes. Do it for me…for us…"

Kataryna felt something. She could not believe it. It was Raven's fingers moving on her leg. "That's it, fight to come back."

†

Raven had been trying to fight her way back for what seemed like an eternity. Then she heard it, the most beautiful sound known to humanity, the voice of love. It surrounded her; it intertwined with her very being. She followed the voice back into her body. The first thing to hit her was the pain. The next was the arms surrounding her. Raven knew who it was without seeing.

Slowly Raven opened her eyes. She was only able to open them halfway, but that did not matter, she felt she had finally come home. No, she knew that could not be right. It would not hurt so much. Anguish ripped across her face.

Kataryna saw the pain and reacted. "Raven, I know you are in pain. You are burning with fever and the tea can help. I need for you to drink it." She picked up the cup. "Please Raven, you have to drink this." She felt Raven's fingers grip her leg. That was Raven's acknowledgment that she had heard her. "Open your mouth, my love."

Slowly Raven parted her lips just a little. Kataryna lifted the cup to her lips and let the cool liquid drizzle down into her mouth. She tilted Raven's head back, making it easier to go down her throat.

Amara watched the interaction of the two women. Both of her mothers had now come home, however there would be many obstacles to overcome. Both of them were stubborn and would fight each other and themselves most of the way, but they would make it. She had faith in them. Amara now wished they had faith in themselves.

Kataryna watched Amara as she silently left the room. Raven slept once more, her head now resting on Kat's left shoulder. She watched her sleep for a bit longer, then laid her own head against the wall and closed her eyes. She lay listening to Raven breathe, contemplating what she would do to the commander.

✝

Never before in his life had Commander Carraig known heart-stopping fear. However, at that moment in time he was panic-stricken. He would do whatever was necessary to save his own life. The commander made a plan while pacing in the room on the second floor of the inn, which he had turned into his command post.

Baylor acknowledged the guards in the hall, knocked, then entered. He had an inkling this was not going to be good, that the commander planned on making him the sacrificial lamb. "Commander Carraig, you sent for me?"

Carraig turned and set about saving his own neck from the noose. Turning to his lieutenant he wove his web of deceit. "Lieutenant Baylor, please sit. Would you like some wine?" He poured some in a goblet, offering it to him.

"Thank you sir, no. I have been informed you have a mission for me, sir. How may I be of service?" Baylor dreaded the words coming. He knew seeing his brother once more would be the death of him. When their parents were brutally slain and the brothers separated at childhood, Baylor had sworn vengeance. Vengeance against the pirates that had stolen their childhoods, even if it meant paying with his life. Baylor sat in front of the desk awaiting his orders.

Carraig rested his right hip on the corner of the desk and appeared to be thinking. He then turned his attention back to Baylor. "Answer me this. Why did you have knowledge and not inform me, your commander?" He made as if to study his manicured fingernails.

Baylor looked confused. "Knowledge of what, sir?"

"Do not deny knowledge of what you knew and yet saw fit not to inform me, your commander. Come now, young man, do you think me a fool as well?" He thought maybe to play the guilt card. "I was under the impression that you and I were friends, that we shared mutual respect."

Baylor now sat in fear on the edge of his chair. "Sir, what do you speak of? What am I to have known?"

Carraig now went in for the kill. He stood and strolled across the room to the window. He watched out the window at the chaos below. "Knowledge that Captain Raven and her crew were under protection of the Dragon. You knew and did not inform me. I consider it not just disrespectful to myself but treason to the Dragon, as does she, Lieutenant. The guards outside will escort you back to the palace as per the Dragon's orders."

Neither of the men heard the door opening or the Dragon slipping quietly into the room. "I gave NO such orders, Carraig!"

Baylor jumped to attention upon hearing the voice. "Sir! Dragon, sir!"

The commander thought quickly to try to come up with a new plan. However, the deadliness in her eyes relayed that he was doomed and his heart plummeted to his boots. He too jumped to attention, trying to fight down the rising nausea.

Kataryna stepped into the room and slammed the door behind her. The breeze created by the rapidly closing door sent papers flying from the desk in all directions. "Lieutenant, please stand down. Also as a matter of record, it is no longer Dragon. It is Queen Kataryna. As for you, Carraig, do not dare try to put the blame for this on anyone but yourself. You are the commander of your ship, are you not?" She glanced from one man to the other. She grasped within a heartbeat what the commander had been scheming.

She knew the commander to be self-preserving; however, she had not thought he would lower himself to this level. "Tell me, Commander, would you have your lieutenant hang in your place?" She saw panic in his eyes.

"Dragon...I mean, I am sorry...Queen Kataryna, I intended no such thing. I take offense at the accusation. I have just learned that my lieutenant knew of your wishes and chose not to inform me. I intended to turn him over to you." His hands shook behind his back as he stood at attention. His courage had momentarily returned.

Kataryna snorted in laughter at the commander's last statement. She slowly dropped her gaze to the floor in front of her feet. She stuck her foot out a little as if studying her boot. "Tell me, Baylor, did you indeed know. Come now, out with the truth, my good man."

Baylor looked her in the eyes when she gazed at him. "No, my Queen, I did not. I would never disobey your orders."

Carraig was outraged that his own man would betray him. He opened his mouth to protest but no words came forth. The Queen's next words stopped any further thought of saving not only his skin, but his life. His fate was sealed.

"I understand your brother is Lorenzo." She stealthily moved her hand to the hilt of her sword.

Baylor's eyes lit up. "Yes, my Queen, he is. I have not laid eyes upon him for many seasons."

"Well then, you are welcome to stay at the palace also for as long as you wish. It would make it much easier for the two of you to get reacquainted." Kataryna had one more thing for him to do though before he could go about his personal business. "I have a mission for you before you retire for the evening. I wish for you to pick the best men you have and arrange to have Captain Raven safely moved to the palace at sunrise. Take care though, if anything were to happen to her, it will be on your head. As for you Carraig…" She turned to him and as she did, she pulled her sword.

Kataryna moved so swiftly the commander could not react in time. Her sword moved through him, opening him up and spilling his insides to the floor. The Dragon lurking inside her stepped forth and exacted her revenge.

The commander looked up from the wound to see the gleam in her eyes. The Dragon was loose once more. He could not stop himself from wetting his trousers as he saw the sword fly toward him once more.

Chapter Ten

Driving the sword through his heart, she screamed her knowledge of events on his ship. "You bastard, you are the one who did that to her! You are the one who beat her, who tried to kill her. Dying is too good for you. May you spend an eternity in Hades for what you have done! Even that is too good for you."

Unfazed by the brutality, Baylor was curious about something. Even as he watched his former commander's body drop to the floor, Baylor could not stop the words from flowing freely. "Queen Kataryna, I do not understand. How did you know?"

The Queen regarded his question. "Know to come here? Know what happened on the ship?"

Baylor nodded.

"Remember I know many things, one of them being my own men. Most of the men upon your ship are loyal to the crown, therefore they report to me. However, if you had left this inn with his men, you would never have made it to the palace still breathing. He gave them orders to kill you, making it look to be as if you were escaping."

Kataryna turned to find Baylor with feet glued to the floor and eyes on the crumpled man. "Fear not Baylor, your fate will not be the same. I have known for some time now that he would never have my interests foremost in his endeavors. You, however, I do trust. You are brother to Lorenzo, who in turn is friend and comrades with Raven. How could I not trust in you, Commander Baylor?" She smiled as she watched the shock overcome him. "Yes Baylor, you are the commander now. So as the commander I have given you a mission, my good man. Now be off with you, I am sure your brother and Gezana will be more than willing to help you. On our way, I will make arrangements to clean up this mess."

Opening the door Baylor found palace guards, not the commander's henchmen. He held the door as Kataryna passed through it. In barely a whisper, he thanked her from his heart. "Thank you, My Queen. My life is yours to command." Still stunned, he turned to face her, bowing with the utmost respect. "Thank you for the trust and faith you have bestowed upon me. I will not disappoint you, My Queen."

Kataryna turned to the palace guards, "There seems to have been an accident. Please remove and dispose of it. Please clean the room and pay the innkeeper for the use of the room. Then report to Captain Raven's room for further orders. Dismissed..." She headed toward Raven's room.

By morning Raven's fever had broken, meaning the medicine had worked. At sunrise, Commander Baylor informed Queen Kataryna that arrangements were made to move Captain Raven to the palace. Unable to watch them move Raven for fear it would cause the captain pain, Kataryna returned to the palace to finalize details there.

Slowly the procession made its way through the town, then up the hill to the palace. Greeting them at the gate, Aiden helped guide Baylor through the palace to the room his mother had chosen.

All through the darkness of the night, Kataryna had prepared the rooms next to hers. Everything was to be perfect for Raven to recover properly. Sitting in her favorite chair, she watched the flames dance in the fireplace before her. A knock at her door, and a voice, brought her back to the present.

"My Queen, the captain and her escorts are here."

Kataryna gathered her thoughts. She thought of all that had led up to Raven's battered body being brought to the palace. Kat knew mistakes had been made by both of them and was sure there would be more in the future. She regretted all the wasted years. Sighing she rose and opened the door. Stepping into the hall, she watched as they carried Raven in; sending a prayer to any God that would listen. "Please let her live, it's all I ask." She opened the door to Raven's room and stepped inside, out of the way.

Amara, Aiden, and Baylor followed behind the men carrying the litter. Not wanting her to suffer during the move, Amara had given Raven a tea that morning with a sleeping potion mixed in. It would not do well in her recovery to physically suffer more if it could be avoided. After Raven was settled Aiden showed Commander Baylor, Gezana and Lorenzo to their rooms. Not one of them had slept the nightfall before as they kept vigil beside Raven and they were now exhausted. They retired until the evening meal.

†

As the sun was preparing to set Aiden knocked on the commander's door first, then Gezana's to inform them the evening meal had been laid out in the smaller dining hall rather than the Great Hall. Kataryna wanted them to feel at home in the more intimate setting. The Great Hall could be intimidating. She joined them a few moments later, with Amara trailing behind her. Immediately upon sitting, a plate heaped with the queen's favorite foods was placed in front of her. However, not a bite was eaten.

By then Kataryna had waited long enough. She needed to see Raven. Amara had made her promise not to disturb the sleeping woman and she had agreed, though she desperately needed to see her now. She looked up to find Amara watching her with a knowing smile upon her face.

Amara watched as her mother grew increasingly agitated. This pleased Amara greatly. Her mother still held feelings for the captain. Amara chuckled knowing it was pure torture for her mother. Finally, she gave in. "Mother, I have had Sairana prepare a tray for Captain Raven, so that you may take it to her. I am sure it is ready by now."

Kataryna was out of her chair like a panther pouncing on its prey. She flew through the door almost knocking Sairana over. She swiftly took the tray from the young girl's hands before she dropped it. "I am truly sorry, Sairana, I did not mean to startle you."

After gathering her wits, Sairana took the tray back from the queen. "'Tis I that am sorry, My Queen, I should have not been standing so closely to the doors." She kept her head bowed.

Kataryna placed a finger under the girl's chin and lifted her head, although Sairana still would not meet the queen's eyes. "Sairana, there is nothing to be sorry for. I was in a hurry and did not watch where I was going. Never apologize for something you did not do. It was my error, not yours." The look of shock evident on the girl's face made Kataryna toss her head back and bellow with laughter. "Yes, I can admit my wrongdoings. It seems I am truly changing. In the past I would have had your head, now I am the one who must beg forgiveness. So, shall we take the captain her evening meal?"

Sairana smiled. She liked this new queen. "Yes, My Queen, let us."

†

Amara was not the only one who had taken notice of Kataryna's agitation. Sitting at the far end of the table was King Theos. Upon his arrival at the palace, Kataryna delegated to Aiden that all were to be informed that her father had returned and he was to be given the respect his title of king deserved.

King Theos had watched, thoroughly amused, as all through the meal the tension on Kataryna's face grew with each passing moment. He loved his daughter, wanting only happiness for her. He knew when she had wed the prince her future was not what it was meant to be. Theos could see the lifelessness in her eyes as she did not wed the one she loved.

Now he saw something different, he saw love. He had witnessed the same love that evening, so long ago when the two had returned to the palace from their adventure. Since then, both women had committed terrible atrocities. All those seasons ago he felt, if they could make it through the dark times to come, they would find each other once more.

†

188

Kataryna slowly opened the door to the inner sleeping chamber. Sairana followed her in with a tray holding broth and tea. Amara had requested that if she needed to disturb her to try to get substance into Raven, she would need it to build her strength back up.

"Sairana, please set the tray beside the bed. I will get as much of it into her as I can." She turned from looking at the sleeping woman to Sairana. After the deaths of Delfina and Thalia several seasons ago, Sairana was the only one allowed to attend her. "Thank you, Sairana, for everything over the seasons. Delfina and Thalia taught you well."

"Thank you ma'am…" She bowed and quietly left, closing the door behind her.

Sairana would not go far. If Kataryna opened the door, she would find Sairana sitting in a chair on the other side of it, awaiting further orders. Sitting on the edge of the bed, she watched Raven breathe. She whispered to the stillness of the room. "If I had lost you…oh, I do not wish to think of it. It hurts too much to think of that."

She smoothed back the hair from Raven's face. Kataryna noticed Amara had carefully washed the blood and debris from her hair and body earlier. "You look so beautiful, now that you do not look as if you have been to Hades and back again."

Beautiful still did not do justice to Raven. She was handsome and almost otherworldly appearing in Kat's eyes. She seemed to be a Goddess sent from the heavens above. Kataryna looked on at her with awe, tears welling in her eyes. "My love, what am I to do? How am I to make you understand? Could you ever understand?"

†

Raven had slept soundly through the day. Her conscious mind floated near the surface. Unbeknownst to Kataryna, Raven had heard her words. She heard them yet did not understand them. She could not comprehend what Kat meant. What would she not be able to understand? Had she missed some vital piece of information while being unconscious?

†

It was not the time, though, for self-recrimination, she needed to help Raven heal. Kat lightly ran her fingers along Raven's jaw. "Darling, it is time to wake up. I need you to drink some of this broth and tea. Raven, come on, you need to return to us." Caressing Raven's bare arm, she felt her stir slightly. "Come now, love, open those eyes, I felt you move, so I know you can hear me. I want you to open those beautiful eyes for me." Raven did just that, opening them completely for the first time since her injury.

Kataryna stood and bent over the bed. "I am going to gently lift you so I may slide you up on the pillows. It will be easier for you to drink without choking." Their eyes met briefly. "Are you ready?"

Raven's throat was dry, her response more of a croak than words. "Yes…ready…"

Wrapping her arms around Raven, she was careful not to touch her wounds. Kataryna fluffed up the pillows as she slid the injured woman into a sitting position. "Okay, which would you like first tea or broth?"

Raven smiled. "Side of cow…"

Kataryna threw her head back, roaring with laughter. She could not contain herself as she continued to laugh,

190

causing tears to appear on her cheeks. "I am sorry, love, I do not mean to laugh at you. I truly am sorry." Finally her laughter subsided. "I must confess, I have not laughed like that in many, many seasons." Under her breath she added, 'fifteen seasons' as she picked up the bowl of broth.

Raven's exceptional hearing picked up the extra words as well as the sadness. "Kat...once I am better we must talk."

"I know we must. I would also like to ask you to stay." She saw the tentative look in Raven's eyes. "I want you to stay, please, for me." Kataryna lifted the bowl for Raven to drink from, tilting it slightly. "As for talking, we have plenty of time for that, now do we not? At this moment I want you think of nothing other than healing. If I was to let you do anything else, Amara would have my head on a pike upon the palace wall." Pulling the bowl away, she found Raven had drained it of most of the broth.

Seeing the expression on Kataryna's face Raven laughed slightly. "I was hungry. I do not think I have eaten in several sunrises. As for the other, I am unsure as to the damage to my ship, so I do not know if we can leave right away or not anyway. If I am to stay here...what of Gezana and Lorenzo?"

Kataryna smoothed the blanket over Raven's body. "They are settled in here at the palace. I have invited them to stay as long as they wish. I also offered them positions within the palace, should that suit them."

Raven seemed shocked. "Have they accepted?" She did not want to appear ungrateful for the offers for herself or them, but she did not want to feel obligated either.

"Both of them informed me that it was your decision and they would abide by it. It seems they would follow you to the ends of the world if you so choose." Picking up the mug of tea she held it up for Raven. "I would be honored if you would choose to stay. I am sure Father would like to see you. He has been asking Amara since you arrived if you had awakened enough for visitors." Kataryna immediately pulled the cup away when Raven choked slightly on the tea. "Please take deep breaths, try not to cough any more than necessary. I fear you might pull stitches."

She saw what she thought to be a flash of fear pass through Kat's eyes. "King Theos is here, in the palace? I did not realize, I thought he was banished to the Wildlands."

Kataryna looked at her tentatively, almost shyly. If they could continue to talk like this, maybe, just maybe they could at least remain friends. Kataryna felt like the shy girl all those seasons ago. She picked a piece of lint off her trousers; trying to keep herself calm. "I had him brought back to the palace a sunrise after you left. I have come to realize I have quite a bit to atone for, starting with my father."

Raven was shocked. Looking away, she gathered her thoughts before speaking. She still could not wrap her mind around that Kataryna might be trying to find her way home. "Why is he truly here, Dragon? What demented plots have you in mind for all of us?"

†

It hurt deeply that Raven would say those words to her, even though she knew she was within her right to say them. At one time, that had been true; she would have had an ulterior motive brewing. Kataryna wanted to do the one thing that came naturally to her…to lash out. Closing her eyes to calm her anger, one thought stormed through her mind. How dare Raven accuse her, when she had bestowed the same wretched fate upon others just as her actions as the Dragon had in the past?

"I understand that you have no trust in me. Alas, I would not trust me either. Trust is to be earned, as is loyalty and honor; all of which I gave away long ago. It came to my attention that you perpetrated similar crimes upon your fellow man as I. I, however, am willing to try. Are you?" Kataryna stood, adjusted her tunic trying to prolong the moment a little longer. She had to do whatever she could to have Raven back in her life.

†

Raven watched as sadness then despair crossed Kataryna's face. Raven's mind worked overtime. Is she truly trying to change or is this some trick? Does she truly want me here? If she does, does she still care for me? No, I cannot fathom that. I do not know what to do. I need to speak with Gezana, he knows these matters more than I. Damn it to Hades, what am I to do? What am I to say? Her mind continued to war within herself. Eventually her mind won over her heart. Raven looked away.

†

What hope the queen had crashed down upon her when Raven neither acknowledged nor replied to her question. She had not expected it, yet longed to receive a spark of hope; or, at the very least, a 'Go to Hades' if nothing else. Silence was worse. Kat would rather have Raven bellow at her than show complete and utter indifference. Without looking back, she made for the door. "I am sure you are in need of sleep. I will bring your morning meal. Amara will be in to check on you before she retires for the evening. Let her know if there is anything you need this night or anything special for your morning meal. Good night."

†

Over the next three sunrises Kataryna brought Raven all her meals and sat with her while she ate. By the second evening Kataryna's ire was at its peak. Had she not given Raven every chance to talk to her? Instead the wounded woman sat on the bed, ate her meals in silence, then fell asleep immediately afterward.

By the third sunrise, the queen had had enough. As all the meals before it, Kataryna set the tray on the table by the bed, but that was the extent of her politeness. "Are you going to ignore me now as you have all the previous times? If so, I think I will take my leave of you. There are items that need my attention that I have let go in order to take care of you, yet you seem not to care whether I am here or not."

Raven lay upon the bed contemplating Kataryna's words. What did she want? Of that, she was still unsure. She wanted to believe in Kat. She wanted more than anything in the known world to believe in the woman she loved. At every meal, Kat would tell her little things which either the children had done while growing up or that had happened to them. Going on faith, she quietly spoke. "I am sorry for the past several meals. I have been deep in thought over the events of the last many nightfalls. Please give me a little more time. I am still in a bit of shock. Do you think it possible I could sit in the chair by the fire while I have my meal?"

Raven was trying so Kataryna decided to stay. "Yes, I think that would be nice. Let me help you up and into the chair, then I will bring you your meal." Gently she helped Raven to stand. After gaining her balance, Kat led her to the chair by the warm fire.

Raven felt as weak as a newborn, which angered her beyond reason. How could she be so weak? Had she not been injured before? Never had she felt so beaten down.

As if reading her love's mind, Kataryna spoke up. "Do not feel defeated, my love. You were gravely injured. It will take well over a full moon for you to truly be up and about. You must heal properly and not push yourself too hard."

Raven looked up at Kat...her Kat, and smiled. The term of endearment wrapped itself around her heart and warmed her. "Thank you for everything. I do not know if I could have survived without your kindness and love. I must, however, be truthful with you as you have with me. I want no part of the Dragon. If Queen Kataryna has truly returned, perhaps we might be friends. I feel each of us are in need of one. After that we see where the Fates take us."

Kataryna thought it must have pained her to admit such a thing. "I should be the one to thank you. It takes a strong being to admit the need of others. I also assure you the queen has returned. There might be moments when I may slip, but I truly hope you are within reach to catch me when I do." She retrieved the tray and sat to help Raven with her meal. It was to be a small step, but it was in the right direction.

It was that one moment that sealed Raven's mind to its task. She had to get to know this dark beauty all over again, as well as try to regain her trust and love. In her heart she knew Kat would do anything for her.

After a few moments, "If you will excuse me, Raven, I unfortunately must go and deal with two mule-headed lords." Kat withdrew from the room to leave Raven to her thoughts.

†

The two that arrived with the dispute were two lords the Dragon had favored because they were so ruthless and would do as she asked. When diplomacy did not work, Kataryna came close to letting the Dragon loose. Mere heartbeats from that happening, the chamber doors opened and King Theos entered.

King Theos pretended to be shocked to find people in the room so late. He, however, had known who was in there and what events were taking place, having been witness to it many times himself. His daughter could not hold back much longer, if the shouting were any sign of the anger in the room. "Oh, I beg pardon. I did not think anyone would be in here this late in the evening." Turning he addressed the lords. Remembering them both as young men, he acknowledged them. "Lord Mayoo, Lord Colton, it is good to see the both of you. It has been many moons since I have had the pleasure."

Each lord bowed out of respect for the king, then they exchanged glances. Lord Colton chose to speak for both. "King Theos, it is good to have you once again in the palace and ruling the lands. These past seasons have been an insightful time."

King Theos smirked. "I must inform you, my lords, that I do not rule these lands. Queen Kataryna rules over all. I also ask of you to bestow upon her the respect you would have upon me. Now I must beg your pardon and take my leave." He bowed to the lords then to Kataryna. "My Queen…till morning then." Knowing they received the message, he strode from the room.

The lords had arrived claiming a dispute over a few head of cattle, but Kataryna knew the real reason behind their visit. They came to see if the tales were true. They tested her, to see if she could be pushed into reverting into the Dragon. In the end, she won and the lords, with their tails between their legs, returned to their homes.

†

Before retiring for the evening Kataryna went to check on Raven once more. The moon had risen long ago and most others were long asleep in the palace. Upon arriving at Raven's door, she heard voices. Quietly she listened. It was her father's voice. This made her smile. Knowing they had respect for one another Kataryna dearly hoped her father would help Raven see that his daughter had indeed changed and did love her. Exhausted from dealing with the lords, she retired to her chambers for the evening. "I'll leave the two to their discussions."

†

Earlier, upon leaving the queen and the lords to solve their differences, Theos had gone to visit the dark-tempered captain. Due to Kataryna being with the lords, Theos found Raven sitting in her outer chamber, reading one of the many books he had brought her.

Since Raven's arrival at the palace, King Theos spent part of each sunrise and sunset with her. The first several were spent reading to the young pirate. The later ones in long talks on life, the seas and what their destinies held.

Raven confided in the older man about her life after leaving Pavlone the first time many seasons ago. His heart ached for what could have been, not just for her but for his daughter as well. Once again, he cursed Renaldo for what he had done. Renaldo's betrayal cut deeper than anything and felt as if it would never heal.

In turn, the king confided in Raven. He told her all of which had taken place since her departure long ago. Her anger at Renaldo matched his. If Renaldo had not already been dead, she would have hunted him and gutted him like the pig he was. Keeping that to herself, she instead told King Theos it had to have been destiny that they separated when they did.

The king was not fooled. Raven's true feelings were a result of the special bond they had formed so long ago. It could never be broken. The Fates wove the lifelines and held it together by the love they both shared for a special queen.

That night's talk turned toward what the future held. Raven was still shy talking to the king of her feelings toward Kataryna; yet she felt he was the only one to understand her turmoil. She had tried to talk to Gezana, but he had already come to like the queen very much. Raven did not want him finding her weak with emotions and if they did leave, she wanted nothing interfering with her command. Raven feared if any of her crew were to find out her true undying love for the queen, they would find her unfit to captain. As a pirate your first love was the sea and nothing else stood in its way. Even though Raven's crew had the utmost respect and loyalty for her, she did not wish to test it; especially if they had to leave this place in a hurry. "King Theos, thank you once again for honoring me with your time." She carefully sat down in the wingback chair in front of the warm fire.

He chuckled as he sat beside her, enjoying the warmth of the fire and nibbling from the plates of food he had brought with him. "Please, it is my pleasure, Captain Raven. Our talks are what I look forward to each new day. Now, tell me why you seem upset. Do you wish to talk about it or should I surmise what it is?"

"Please, call me Raven. At this point I do not seem to be the captain of anything." Raven stalled for another moment, afraid to express what she had been thinking prior to when he knocked on her door.

The king nodded. "Then you must call me Theos. Or better still, please call me Father. I feel you could use one at this moment in your life. I know that you are close to Gezana and Lorenzo of your crew; however, there are things you cannot and should not discuss with them. No matter what we discuss, you could never look weak in my eyes. Remember I have borne witness to many things in my lifetime." He saw hesitation in her eyes.

"Thank you for your friendship, Theos. You are correct, there may be a thought or two that…cannot be broached with my men. There may also be one or two that no one could understand or comprehend. Some things I have done no man nor woman should know of, for they would have ill feelings for me if they knew." With head hung low, she silently asked for understanding.

Theos knew of all that she had done. What she did not tell him, he learned from her two friends. He knew and understood she was capable of great evil, yet she also was compassionate, caring, and loving. All of those things made up who and what she was. "Raven, you must understand one thing before all else, my child. You cannot have the good

199

without evil. One cannot exist without the other. Nature would be off balance. Inside yourself you have both as well. If one were to outweigh the other..." Theos hesitated, gathering his emotions. He had always liked Raven from the first moment he met her. "You would be off balance. I feel deep within my bones that both of you have been as such for many seasons now. You each need the other to bring it back. Without balance is to merely exist; to have it is to live. It is time that both of you start on that path." He sipped from the tankard of ale that he had brought with him to Raven's room.

Raven shifted in her chair. "I have done such evil things. I do not know how you can even want me in your palace, knowing what I am capable of."

He set his mug on the table between them. "I do not think you are evil. You have done terrible things yes, but no more than my own flesh and blood. However, they can be put right."

Tears formed in Raven's eyes. "No, they can never be put right. I have killed many men. I also have...I have..." She could not bring the words to her lips.

Theos took her cold hand in his. Even the heat from the fire did not warm her. "To put things right, is to change oneself, to not continue to do the same deeds as before. Do not fear telling me anything, little one. I do not judge you. You yourself have done enough of that for all of our lifetimes."

Raven sighed. "It is not just the men I have killed that haunt me. 'Tis the...oh, Gods...'tis the women I used for my own pleasure. It is the women I have taken against their wills, the virginity I have stolen from many of them. These things I can never make right. They are a part of me. I cannot and will not ask another to share in what I am." Raven's heart was ready to burst from her chest through the pain.

How could she expect him to understand that she felt she had no future to offer Kataryna?

Her thoughts were as clear as a new day dawning. "You have much to offer the woman you love, never doubt that. Have you not started on your journey to lay right the wrongs, by feeling remorse? If you know what you did was wrong and set about not to do those deeds again, then have you not changed your course? Have you not settled your debt? Both of you must look forward, never to return to the past. Your past holds nothing for you now. As for everything else, none of it matters. Kataryna is your destiny; as soon as you accept that you will be able to forgive yourself." King Theos picked up the plates with cheese, bread, and fruit on it that they had only nibbled at up to this point. "Now let us have our snack, I am starving from too much thinking."

Both shared laughter, finishing the food before discussing the book she was currently reading.

✝

Over the next two moons, Kataryna pampered Raven. She brought her meals to her until she was strong enough to walk to the dining hall. Even then, she kept a close eye on Raven to be sure she did not tire too rapidly. Once she was stronger Kataryna escorted Raven on walks through the gardens.

Raven's strength returned as well as her itch to be on the seas once more, yet something held her back. Did she truly wish to return to the cold waters that were once her home, to return to the life of a pirate? If she followed her heart, Raven knew it would remain here by Kat's side, where she would put down her life for her if need be.

Once again, her stubbornness and pigheadedness won over what she truly should do. Instead, her mind convinced her that Kataryna was better off without her. She was a pirate, not good enough to be the consort of a queen. If she were to stay that was all she could ever be. She felt the lords would never see her fit to rule by the queen's side. Raven, therefore, chose to do the only thing she could; she chose to push Kat away.

†

That morning Kataryna dressed in a beautiful sapphire-colored dress she'd ordered the seamstress to make several sunrises before. She still wore her leather breeches and leather boots under the dress. They were familiar to her.

Upon seeing Kat in the dress, Raven was taken back many seasons, to a much younger woman and a much happier time. Even with this vision before her, Raven held her resolve to do what she thought she must. They approached the bench by the water fountain on the far end of the gardens. Raven motioned to the bench. "May we sit and talk?"

The hairs on the back of Kataryna's neck stood on end. Something was wrong, but she could not comprehend what. Everything had been going wonderfully up until this morning when Raven had seemed withdrawn and edgy. Kat sat next to her with her hands in her lap. She then turned to Raven, wondering what was taking place. Kataryna had not even felt this afraid when she had laid eyes upon Raven's battered body, for she knew Amara would not let her die.

"Kat, I feel it is necessary to inform you of my decision to return home at sea." Raven moved her shaking hand so Kat could not see.

Kataryna could not hide the disappointment. "Are you not happy here? I thought maybe we were getting closer once again, that maybe your feelings for me were returning to what they had once been."

Raven closed her eyes. She let out the deep sigh contained within her. "I am sorry if I have led you to feel more than my friendship. I have never meant to harm you. I must, however, tell you that I...that I have a lady awaiting my return. I am truly sorry." Raven watched tears form in Kat's eyes. Her heart broke for the second time in her life.

Kataryna turned from her so as not to let Raven see the tears. She did not want to appear weak. She stood, walked to the fountain and touched the surface of the water, causing a ripple to pass through it. Kataryna then touched the water again causing another ripple to crash into the previous one. The queen felt all warmth leave her body. Something had just been stolen from her, yet she could not name it. "We are like those ripples...always to be crashing into one another, yet never fully being together. I wish you luck on returning home, have a safe journey. Please let Aiden know what supplies you will need. He will have them brought to your ship."

Without turning back, she walked away.

"Kat, please wait..."

The queen held up her hand, stopping Raven in her tracks. "No...I beg you, take your leave of my presence as soon as time allows. I am ashamed and embarrassed enough. Please do not cause me more."

Raven left to search for her crew and Aiden to inform them of her plans. Her crew would not question her, but Aiden would balk. He would then, of course, inform Amara, who would rail against her.

✝

Kataryna fled from the gardens, returning to her chambers. She felt heartache like nothing she knew before. She was not angry with Raven, but with herself for caring so much about the woman. She stormed through the doors to find Amara already in her chambers. Pushing past her daughter to her inner chamber, her anger boiled over. In her anger, Kat shoved Amara to the ground as she pushed past her. Her anger no longer with just herself, it was directed at all. "It did not take you long to hear the news of Raven's departure. I should never have listened to any of you. I should never have thought for one moment that there could ever be any feelings between us. I am who I am and she is a pirate who belongs on the seas. She is returning home and to the whore that is waiting for her." She saw the look on Amara's face at her last words.

The venom in her mother's voice assaulted Amara's ears.

"I am sorry if my words offend you, Amara, you had better take leave of me before I speak words that you may never be able to forgive." The queen removed her dress, needing to revert to what came naturally to her now. Not able to work the bodice buttons, she tore the dress from her body, leaving her standing in her breeches.

Amara watched on as buttons flew across the room and material ripped. She waited until her mother pulled on her crimson tunic and was strapping on her sword belt before venturing to voice her thoughts. Just as Amara tried to speak, her mother turned to her.

"NO! Not a word...I am tired of talking...of feeling. It is too late, too late for any of us. Take this disgusting dress and burn it. I never wish to see it or any like it again within this palace." Handing the dress to Amara, she changed her mind. Pulling her dagger from its hiding place, Kataryna shredded the dress. She then handed her daughter the strips of fabric.

This time Amara feared for her mother's sanity. The Dragon had reared its evil head and was threatening to gain control once more.

"Tell me this, daughter, how could she do this to me? How could she? How could she come here and give me hope. Or was it all in my head, that she cared one way or the other?" She fired the questions off one on top of the other, never giving her daughter time enough to get one word in.

Putting her sword in its scabbard, Kataryna turned toward the door. "Never mind, it matters not. Go help your brother make sure she is under way by sunset, for if she does not leave this port she will surely hang." Leaving her chambers, she went in search of her father.

Amara knew in her heart Raven was lying, so she went in search of her to find out why. She questioned several of the guards as to the location of the captain and her own brother. Being informed that they were at the docks, she set off in that direction. The young healer arrived to find food supplies being loaded on to the ship and the sails being hoisted.

Raven did not need see her; but instead could feel Amara's presence.

†

Amara boarded the ship, walked up to Raven and slapped her hard across the face. So shocked by the action

Raven could do nothing but break down in tears as she dropped to her knees in front of her daughter.

Amara looked first at her hand, then at the kneeling, sobbing woman. Never before had she resorted to violence. It shamed her to do so now, when Raven needed only her love and understanding. "I am sorry. I do not know what came over me. Never before have I lifted so much as a finger in aggression. I am ashamed and will accept whatever justice you decide I deserve."

Raven looked up at Amara with a tear-streaked face as her body shook. Her humiliation was now complete. She had driven this innocent young girl to go against all that she stood for. "It is I that am ashamed, my daughter. I have taken something from you that I can never give back. I have taken your innocence from you. I have made you commit a vile act; which adds to my shame even more. It is not you who deserves punishment, it is I." She laid her head in her hands and continued crying.

Raven's crew watched in awe as their captain crumbled. Several moved to help her but Gezana raised his arm to stop them. This was something none of them could help her with. She had to travel this path alone. Raven's atonement was hers and hers alone.

Amara pulled her partially up into an embrace. Wrapping her arms around her, she gave the captain her love and warmth. In the process, she also gave her a home to come back to. Now it was just a matter of making her feel worthy of it. "Why did you lie? Do you not feel the love within you for my mother? Your love is on display for all to see. I know it...as does Aiden, your crew, even our people can see it in the aura that surrounds you. Do not destroy what is not yours to destroy. The Fates and Goddesses have brought you home. Trust in them. Trust in your soul. She awaits you." Amara pulled Raven to her feet, which shocked all watching. Amara was just a petite slip of a young girl, yet she was able to pull the much bigger woman up as if she were a feather.

✝

Something… a warmth…perhaps life itself exploded within Raven. She could not leave, not now, not ever. It was her destiny to be on land beside her queen. She would remain in any capacity her queen saw fit.

Both of the women heard the startled gasps around them and laughed.

Raven hugged Amara speaking into her ear. "Please find my Queen and inform her I wish to speak with her." She patted the girl on her behind to send her on her way.

"Gezana, stop preparations, we might be staying a little longer." Cheers erupted from all including Aiden.

Aiden stepped closer to her. "Well, it is about time you realized your error. Welcome home, Captain, welcome home."

Raven placed a hand on his shoulder. "We will see, Aiden. The first thing I have to do is beg someone's forgiveness. We will then see what lies ahead for all of us. Please call me Raven."

A short time later, a messenger arrived with word from the palace. Raven was to come at once to speak with the queen.

Raven's crew watched quietly as she read the parchment. Upon smiling, they all let out the breaths they had been holding. "Gezana, it appears that I am needed at the palace. Please take over here for me. It seems it is time for me to grovel at the hands of the Fates. Wish me luck, old friend, I think I am going to need it."

He patted her hard on her back. "All of us grovel at one time in our lives, my old friend. Now be off with you. Just be careful not to scrape your knees too badly." Gezana's boisterous laughter made its way even below deck.

Making her way along the deck Raven looked back. "You are enjoying this way too much, are you not?" With a smile on her face, her words were meant in fun. If she was not mistaken, she thought she saw what appeared to be a twinkle in Gezana's eyes.

"Oh yes, that I am. Now be off with ya, to pay your dues." With his hands, he made a shooing motion as if he was talking to a small child.

"Fine, fine…I will go pay my penance. As for the rest of ya, stay out of trouble till my return." Raven started on her way, thinking of how she was going to get herself out of the mess she had put herself into. Raven knew this was of her own creation. If only she had been more forceful all those seasons ago, none of this would ever have had to happen. Yet, maybe it was the fate of all that they be in this place, in this time, and those were the paths they were all truly meant to take to come to this place in time.

†

Amara greeted Raven upon her arrival at the palace gates. It did not slip by Raven unnoticed that all eyes were upon her. Some held hatred toward her, others held pity. It was the ones that held laughter that she glared back at and watched as they turned away from her. Amara's eyes held laughter as well.

"You too would laugh at me, little one?" She meant to sound forceful, however it came across weakly.

"I would not, if not for your looking as a spanked puppy asking for forgiveness from its master." Amara gasped, the words had escaped without thought.

Raven drew Amara into a hug. "Do not worry, child, 'tis how I feel too. Now show me to her, so I may take my punishment, like the puppy I am."

Each laughed till tears flowed freely.

†

Outside the heavy oak door of the war room Raven listened for a moment to a voice shouting in anger. It could only be one person, the Dragon had returned. She turned her head looking down at Amara. "What have I done?" Raven drew a deep breath and summoned all her courage. "The events that are taking place, I set in motion. It is now time to set all back on the right path." Raven pushed open the doors with a forcefulness she had not used in many moons. She knocked over the two guards standing on the other side of the doors.

Inside, all motion stopped while everyone turned at the intrusion. Two sets of eyes met and held. Neither woman could look away. Raven tempted the Fates. With an even-tempered voice she spoke. "Everyone out…"

As Kataryna was about to object, she watched as Raven's eyes softened from anger to love.

Everyone rapidly left the room, several of them gladly running to make their exit.

Raven dropped to one knee and lowered her head. "I have come to beg my Queen's forgiveness for my stupidity and arrogance."

209

†

The action stunned Kataryna. To see one so strong, not just in body but in mind and soul, bow before her and beg for forgiveness amazed her. It also changed something in her forever. She knew then that this was meant to be, this was where the two of them belonged. Kataryna could not show weakness. The need to throw herself at Raven's feet begging her own forgiveness was so great, that she shook. She had to be strong for Raven, to let her say what she had come to say. She stood in front of Raven's kneeling form. "There has been much of that on both our parts."

Without looking up, Raven bared her soul. "I fear I have been the worse of the two. I have lied to you when you have shown truthfulness. I have shown less than companionship when you have shown only love and compassion. I have been the weaker and have let past actions rule, not destiny or the love that I truly hold within myself for you."

It was then that Kataryna realized Raven had lied about another woman. Raven had to do this on her own; she had to confess what she had done. Knowing that, Kataryna waited, the sadness in her love's face tearing at her heart. It hurt a little though, knowing Raven had once again lied to her. It hurt that Raven had no faith in her, in them.

In order for them to come full circle, Kat would need to let go of her own hurt and pain. She knelt in front of the captain. Sitting back on her feet, she pulled Raven's hands into her lap. "In what do I need to forgive you of, my Captain?"

Raven's head raised, she saw nothing but love and devotion in the eyes that bore into her soul. Her heart spilled

210

forth. "My Queen, I have lied to you. I have no other waiting for me. I have been with many others, but I have loved no other, only you…if you can find it within yourself to forgive me, I will never be with another, never touch another, till I breathe my last breath. I will live only for you, as I have always."

Tears wet both faces as hearts laid open.

Kataryna spoke for both without realizing. "We must have faith and trust in each other. We have already lost so much. Too many seasons have been spent apart from each other. We must not let this happen ever again. I cannot say there will never be a raised voice, but we must not walk away in anger or lie to one another. This is what is in my heart. Is it not the same for yours?"

Each wrapped their arms around the other and was welcomed home after a lifetime of being lost.

†

The queen and her companion spent the next several sunsets sharing all the unspoken secrets. Still each of them held back the worst of the past evil deeds. They leisurely strolled the gardens, walked the docks and beaches conversing on every subject that came to mind. Most evenings after their meal, they sat in Kataryna's outer chamber before the roaring fire in each other's arms. They sat in quiet solitude each night, enjoying the other's company before retiring for the evening.

Each knew a night would come when neither would be able to part from the other. The nights became harder and harder to bear alone. As they parted company one evening Raven resolved what she must do.

With arms wrapped around Kat's waist, she lowered her head kissing her gently. Afterward Raven's heart told her if they did not part company for the evening, they would not until the next morning. The liquid fire flowing between her legs, wetting her trousers only proved what she already knew. "My love, will you join me for a picnic tomorrow?" Raven smoothed back a lock of hair that had fallen onto Kat's face.

It was at that moment each realized the other was wooing them.

Not able to keep her emotions quiet, Kataryna spoke up. "Why, Captain…are you wooing me? Do you think my heart can be swayed by wooing and a picnic?" Kat was in a playful mood and could not help but tease Raven.

Seeing the smile, told Raven that Kat was teasing her. In that, she decided to play along. "Is it working? Am I wooing you correctly, my Queen? Do I need to try harder? Perchance I need to kiss you here?" Raven placed a kiss below her left ear. The skin felt heated to her lips, which drove her on. "…or perhaps here?" Her lips kissed further down her neck. Raven could not hold back. "…or here my love…" The top two buttons on Kataryna's tunic were undone and Raven moved to take advantage of the sight before her. She kissed between Kat's exposed breasts. "…My love…"

Kat had to be the stronger of the two, to do what Raven could not. "Raven, please, we must stop. If you do not, I fear neither of us will be able to. We still have much to talk about." Kataryna shooed Raven back to her own chamber and cold bed for the evening.

✝

The next afternoon found two halves of a whole sharing a picnic in the same meadow where they had first met. Raven spread a blanket next to the rock Kataryna had been sitting on when she had first laid eyes upon her. Raven then laid out the feast she had packed that morning in the kitchen.

Kataryna smiled, knowing Raven wanted this to be special. Part of her feared the reason why. So much was still unsaid between the two of them. Could each accept the other knowing what they had done? Knowing the time was at hand, Kat closed her eyes. Her thundering heart threatened to beat out of her chest any moment.

They both lay on the blanket lost in their own thoughts for quite some time.

Raven sat up turning to Kataryna. She steeled her resolve, setting about the task that she had brought them out here for. "Kat, I have something to ask of you. Actually, I have two things to ask of you. The first is to listen and I beg not judge me. The second will come later. Can you do this?" Raven tried to still her shaky nerves.

Kataryna nodded as words escaped her for the moment.

"Before I dare ask of you, the second one, you must know all of me." When Kat went to speak Raven put her fingers to her lips. "No. Please let me do this." Raven briefly closed her eyes and sighed. "I have done things I am now ashamed of, that others will look down upon. They will tell you I am evil, that I need to be hanged by the neck for my deeds. In that, they are correct. The evil I have forced upon others is unforgivable. You and you alone can forgive me these crimes." She looked up into Kataryna's eyes, falling once more into the love they held for her.

Still looking into Kat's eyes, Raven spoke from her heart. "I have lived the life of a pirate and all that comes with that. I have killed. I have sunk many, many ships. I have looted and plundered those ships and many more." As tears fell, Raven confessed her worst sins of all. "I have…" She faltered, not knowing if she could go on. It was then Raven felt her hand being lifted and placed upon the other's chest. "I have done what no other should do to another. I have taken women against their will. I have taken not just their hopes and dreams but the virginity from some. When they begged for me to stop…I…by the Gods…their begging would only add to the fire I felt. I became what I hated the most. I can truly understand if you wish for me to leave your company. I do hope you can see me for who I am now, not who I was." Raven laid open her heart and soul. It was Kataryna's turn to accept her or send her away.

Kataryna's tears matched the ones coating Raven's face. The queen spoke from her soul. "My love, we start fresh here in this meadow where we first met so long ago. You must first have forgiveness in yourself. As for me, I love you, all of you. Your past is what makes your future…our future."

Venom snaked its way into Raven's words. "How can I forgive myself for what I have done?"

Kat squeezed Raven's hands. "How can you not? Have you not resolved to change? Have you not pledged your heart to me?" Kat watched as a smile formed on Raven's face. "See, there is good in you. You could never give your love and not be a kind and loving woman. I see how you smile at Amara and Aiden, as if they were your own children. There is good and evil in all of us. I too have done unspeakable things. I too have had to ask forgiveness from many. I will continue to do so with my people for many

Once Upon a Time

seasons to come." Pulling Raven down to her, their lips met and love flowed. This time neither stopped the other.

†

If one were to come through the meadow, they would have borne witness to clothes being carefully discarded. They then would have known what the Fates meant by destiny and love.

Raven was in awe of Kat's body, pausing a moment to catch her breath. Never had she seen any other as beautifully breathtaking. Knowing she had never reacted this way to another being in her life, Raven was momentarily thrown. Kat was as muscular as her, yet was all feminine woman.

Kissing Kat's neck Raven had to slow herself down for fear of exploding into a million pieces. Her mind and body both on overdrive, she took a deep breath. She lay featherlight kisses upon the inviting chest below her, lingering near Kat's nipple. Feeling her lover squirm below her would have been enough to spur her on but Kat's words made her pulse quicken even more.

"Please, my love, take me, please."

Raven smiled. "As you request, for I live to please you." Wanting to tease Kat just a little, she moved her lips away from her breast and kissed her arm. "What would you like of me first, darling?"

Kat gently put her hands upon Raven's head and moved it back to her breast. "Please they hunger for you, as does my whole being. Please suck them."

Unable to resist her, Raven licked the nipple in front of her face as her right hand found the other and caressed it. She then switched and repeated the pleasures on the opposite

215

one. Repeating the move several more times, she watched as Kat's nipples grew larger. Amazed at the size they became she finally sucked on one.

Kat's hand that had been on the back of her head grabbed a handful of her hair and held her tight to her breast.

"Raven, my love, you are driving me wild. More, please more."

Raven gave in to what her lover wanted. She bit down hard on one as she pinched and pulled on the other. Kat's hips came up from the ground causing her wet center to rub against Raven's hard clit. The move caused Raven to almost explode on contact. She didn't want that, not yet at least. In her heart she wanted to please Kat first, she herself could wait.

"Love, you must not do that. Loving you is what matters to me at the moment." Raven took Kat's nipple between her teeth and held it there. Her right hand lightly moved over her lover's hip then lower to find Kat's clit. As she bit the hard nipple she pinched the engorged clit just as hard.

"Raven...so wonderful. So good. Can't hold it much longer." Kat could feel it building in her center, its hot spasms moving outward.

Sensing Kat's oncoming orgasm, she pinched the clit hard again then slid two fingers inside. Gently she pulled them out and reentered her lover. Raven wanted their first time to be gentle and loving because there would be time later for raw unleashed passion to flow between them. This, however, they would look back to over the years and remember the first love that flowed between them. Or so she thought, because she was about to find out that Kat had different ideas.

"Yes please, please, inside harder." Kat was wild with passion. She needed Raven to possess her, to take her hard and leave her mark upon her. Much to Kat's dismay, Raven continued her gentle lovemaking.

Moments later Kat could take it no longer. "Raven, now. You cause me to beg of you. Take me, fuck me hard and make my body yours as you have my soul."

Raven's body reacted without thought as she thrust her fingers harder into Kat. Pulling out she pushed harder the next time, leaving her fingers lingering inside. Raven could feel the first spasms around her fingers.

"Yes, love, yes more." Kat held Raven's head to her breast with her right hand while she pinched her other nipple with the left.

Watching Kat touch herself excited Raven more, causing her to pull out of Kat's wet center and start ramming rapidly in and out.

Kat's eyes closed and her head tilted back as her orgasm shook her body causing her to bellow. "By the Gods, yes! Harder…more!"

Raven took her as hard as she dared for fear of hurting her.

Lifting her head up, Kat pulled Raven's head up so she could look into her eyes as she came. "Raven, love…harder. I beg you. You will not hurt me, harder!"

"As you wish." Raven pulled out of her, causing Kat to gasp at losing the connection. She maneuvered herself so that she was kneeling between Kat's legs. "Hold your legs spread open for me, love."

Kat took hold of behind her knees and pulled her legs up and as far apart as she could. This caused her center and ass to be displayed beautifully and Raven told her so.

Raven licked her lips at the sight displayed for her taking. Sitting back on her legs, Raven stared in awe. She wanted Kat completely, but would Kat want that as well? "Oh my, Kat, how beautiful you are for me. I want them both. May I?"

"Yes please, yes. Take all of me."

Feeling her own needs building to the breaking point, Raven did her best to ignore them. Instead, she leaned forward and thrust three fingers of one hand into Kat as she took her lover's ass with the thumb of the other hand.

Feeling Raven's thumb enter her ass and the others pounding into her, Kat could hold the oncoming orgasm no longer. She came hard and fast, bellowing out Raven's name for all the Gods to hear.

"Raven...by all the Gods..."

When one orgasm subsided another overtook her as Raven didn't slow down her relentless pounding into the woman screaming her name.

Finally coming down from the last orgasm that overtook her entire body, Kat had need of one thing—Raven under her begging for release.

Raven had been hovering over her princess kissing her breasts when she suddenly found herself being pushed onto her back. Kat then grabbed one of her nipples with her teeth and bit hard. "Kat, yes!"

While biting down hard on her nipple, Kat found Raven's hard clit and pinched as hard as she could.

Needing something to anchor herself, Raven clutched at the blanket that lay beneath them. If she had grabbed Kat's arms with such force she was afraid she might have hurt her. When she heard the blanket tear slightly Raven knew she had made the right choice.

That was the last rational thought she was to have for a while as Raven found herself being flipped onto her stomach and her lower body lifted into the air.

Kat pushed Raven's legs apart as she ran her fingers through the flowing river of wetness she found between her love's legs. "May I, love? May I have you?"

Raven now on her hands and knees waiting to be taken could barely speak. "Yes, please. Take what has always been yours only to take."

At Raven's words Kat entered her just as her pirate had entered her. She found her lover's entrance to be tight as a virgin's, but she kept thrusting faster anyway. The more she did the more Raven opened up letting Kat enter her with three fingers. Then she felt it when she thrust as deep as she could.

By the Gods, she's a virgin. How? Why? Kat hesitated a moment as the knowledge set in.

Kat didn't want to embarrass her so she said nothing, only continued to take what was being offered to her.

Raven felt Kat stop for a moment as she felt a slight pain inside as Kat's fingers thrust deep. Afraid Kat would stop she urged her on.

"Kat, love, please, I am about to explode. I cannot hold it back. Please fuck me, brand me as yours."

"I will, my pirate. Reach under yourself and pinch your clit. Pinch it as I fuck you completely. What I'm about do might hurt at first, my love, but it will be worth it. I promise you."

Raven reached under herself and grasped the hard bundle of nerves. Pinching hard, she'd let Kat do whatever she wanted to her at that moment. "Do it, I don't care. Do it!"

Kat pulled out of both places. She coated her whole left hand with Raven's wetness and some of her own. Then put some on the first two fingers of her right hand. Folding her thumb into her palm she pushed her right hand into Raven's center as she entered her ass with the two fingers of the other hand.

Feeling her lover entering her all at once was incredible. Then suddenly Kat's hand wasn't stopping at just the few fingers entering her, she pushed hard into her causing Kat's whole hand to plunge inside. Never feeling anything as incredible as this, it turned the pain she felt into ecstasy. Her hand left her clit as she needed both to hold herself up so that she might continue to receive Kat's wonderful gifts.

"Oh Gods yes! I'm coming…please."

Kat pulled out slightly then pushed as deep as she possibly could into her. The walls around her hand started to spasm as she felt Raven's body begin to shake.

"Kat! Gods, never before…don't stop. Never stop!" Raven felt her being explode from within. She could not stop the scream that started until it left her throat raw and useless.

Collapsing onto the blanket facefirst Raven could do nothing to stop the tears that flowed. She let them fall freely, as free as she now felt in her soul. It finally dawned on her that this is what she had been waiting for her whole life. To be completely and utterly filled to the point of oblivion by the one that she loved more than her own life itself.

After wiping her hands, Kat lay beside her true love. Pulling Raven into her arms, she became Raven's lifeline until she completely relaxed.

Soon the couple lightly dozed in the afternoon sun as the gods and goddesses gazed down upon them smiling.

Sometime later, lying in each other's arms, completely sated for the first times in their lives, Raven asked her second request of Kataryna. "Kataryna, Kat, my Queen...would you do me the honor of being my wife?" She watched as shock and fear overcame Kat's face. Raven sat up, reaching for her tunic that lay discarded on the grass. She felt an overwhelming need to run as far and fast as she could.

"Raven, love, please...I am...Oh Hades...I am afraid. Please, I do love you. I do want a life with you. I just need time to absorb all of this. Please, I ask of you to give me time."

Raven knew Kataryna loved her, she heard it in her words. She had felt it as they made love. It had been only a momentary lapse. Raven's heart sang as it dawned on her that she had not said no, only that she needed time. Throwing her tunic across the grass, she descended upon Kat. Moments later the goddesses whom watched over them smiled as they bore witness to each worshipping the other's body, gently causing pleasure so sweet they knew nothing in life could compare.

†

As they dressed, Kat asked the question that had plagued her mind the last part of the afternoon. "My love, I must ask—and please do not take this other than I am curious—has no lover pleased you in the manner I have this day?"

The shy blush that came over Raven's face took Kataryna aback.

Raven spoke from the long untouched depths of her heart. "No. I never craved another's touch in either of those places. Yet I have longed to feel you completely and utterly filling all of me since I laid my eyes upon you once more.

221

Now I do not know if I could ever be satisfied enough. Even as we speak I have need of your wondrous gifts once more."

The love in Kat's heart blossomed all the more for her pirate. Feeling as if she walked in the clouds among the gods, Kat placed upon Raven's lips the most delicate of kisses. "I thought it not possible to love you more than I already do, but I must admit I find myself wrong. Instead, I find that I love you more with every new thing I am learning of you. You have caused my heart to stutter and swell that you saved such a wonderful gift for me. I have no thoughts on how I could ever return such a gift."

"Kataryna, *my princess*, you only need love me. That is all I could ever ask for in this life and beyond." Raven kissed Kat's hand as she helped her up on her horse.

Riding back to the palace each felt soreness, yet wonderful. The sun was setting when they arrived at their home. Kataryna bid Raven good evening, which Raven did not take to heart. Her lover needed time and Raven herself wanted a long soak in a hot bath to soothe the soreness between her thighs.

Kataryna left Raven to retire to her chambers as she went in search of her father. Kat found him sitting in his favorite chair reading as he did almost every night. She winced as she gingerly sat on the floor beside his chair, just as she had in her youth.

The King smiled, he knew that look. Raven had come to him that morning and asked for Kataryna's hand in marriage. He was overcome with joy and broke down, telling her that she was making an old man very happy. The day in the meadow had obviously been a very good one. He chuckled as he thought of Raven having the same trouble with sitting. "So, little one, we have all finally found our way, have we not?" He stroked her hair, just as he had when she was a child.

"Oh Papa, I do love her. Do you think it is selfish of me to want a life with her? I am Queen, I must think of our people. What are they to think of a pirate for a ruler?" Her body was content even though her heart warred with her head as she laid her head on his knee.

"Listen to me, my daughter. You must do what is in your heart. You must do what you could not so many seasons ago. She is your destiny as you are hers. Now, I wish to sleep the night away, knowing you both are safely back, within the palace walls. I also know that you wish for a long soak in a hot bath to relieve the soreness."

Her head snapping up, Kat looked mortified.

"Oh please, my child…'tis nothing new to me. Now get with you. I will see you at sunrise or possibly a little later if you wish to sleep longer."

Kat smiled. She knew what she had to do. Calling for Aiden and her messengers, the Queen sent out parchments to all her lands. Until all was set in place Kat remained secluded in her chambers to steel her courage for what had to be done.

†

Four sunrises later the morning sun brought with it chaos as lords and their guards descended upon the palace. All came in response to the messages Aiden sent to each of the lands. The day was spent preparing lodging for all the extra people each of the lords had brought with them. A special evening meal was planned with great care.

Kataryna had Aiden inform each of them nothing would be discussed until after they ate. She was the only one who knew her plans for the evening festivities. What a plan it was…it was sure to cause much talk throughout all her lands.

All those gathered in the great hall sat enjoying their food. Kataryna was so nervous she did nothing but push the food around on her plate. Finally she motioned for someone to take it away.

The queen rose from her chair at the head of the table. To her right sat Pelor, who had returned that sunrise from Baul. It had been several seasons since he had been within the palace and yet it all felt the same as it did in their youth. To her left sat Raven and next to each of them sat her children. At the opposite end of the long table sat King Theos. Kataryna looked to her father, their eyes meeting.

King Theos nodded his approval, for he knew in his heart what she had decided upon. He truly hoped his smile would give her some strength to make it through the ordeal.

Picking up her goblet Kataryna pounded it upon the table once. When none paid attention, she resorted to one of her old tactics to get attention. In a heartbeat, she jumped upon the table bellowing for all to see and hear. "QUIET!" She stood on the table and looked down the length of it.

All became deadly silent. Jumping from the table she looked at the stunned crowd gathered at the table. "Now that I finally have your attention, I have something to announce for all to hear." She turned to Raven. Kat motioned for the guard at the door. He approached, handing her a scabbard and sword.

Seeing that it was Kat's own sword that the guard was handing her, Raven did not understand what was going on.

Removing the sword from the scabbard, Kat spoke from the heart. She turned it over, presenting the sword to Raven. "Raven, my love, I give to you my trust, my love, and my life. All that I am is yours. The answer is yes. To all, bear witness, I willingly give all that I am to this woman here and now. From this moment in time on, she will be known as Lord Raven, my wife. She will not only rule by my side, but in my place, if the need ever be. Any that feel it their place to argue please do so now and get it over with, because we have a wedding to plan."

†

The great hall remained silent a moment longer, then erupted in cheers. No man, nor woman, would ever raise question to the union. If any one of them did not accept the pairing, they kept it to themselves, for fear of the outcome. Each lord returned to their lands to await an invitation to the wedding and to search for the wedding gift they felt would hopefully gain them favor in the Queen's and new Lord's eyes.

Unfortunately, not one of the lords could grasp that no gift could ever tear their eyes from each other. Raven was the only gift Kat would ever need and likewise for Raven. To each of them the wedding was nothing more than a formality for their people to watch, for both of them already felt in their souls as wed.

They needed no words, no parchment to seal their love. The Fates had already made sure that no man, nor woman, or sword would come between them. There, however, would need to be paid a price for such happiness. When the Fates would ask for it none of them knew.

225

Finale

Destiny

The queen looked down upon the sleeping twin girls. They had fallen asleep only moments into the bedtime story, now she sat gazing at them in wonder. They looked like angels. She and her lord knew better. When they were awake, chaos reigned. It was a happy chaos for the entire palace, as well as their lands. Kat also counted each of the past six seasons as a blessing since these two were born. Each new sunrise brought about a new adventure within the palace walls. The last several moons the twins became more excited at the prospect of having younger siblings.

In the past seven seasons, many things changed under the rule of Queen Kataryna and her Lord. The Goddesses and Fates had watched over them. Upon seeing the love between the two women and what they had gone through to be together, they blessed Kat and Raven with twin girls. As the girls had been born, the God of War could not help but throw a smidgen of his own personality into them and both Kat and Raven could see it in each of them. They could hear it as well when the girls would run down the hallways giggling with Pelor or one of the kitchen staff chasing after them.

†

As the sun set causing the sky to turn a crimson red, the palace was in a flurry to get ready for the two newest arrivals. Amara herself oversaw every detail and patiently waited in their chambers for her parents return. The time was at hand for the birth of her newest siblings. Amara knew in her soul these two would be so very different than Rhiannon and Flora. She looked out the window to the sky. Amara knew what the blood-red sky meant. The Goddesses had once more blessed her mothers with children. This time, however, the God of War was to take what was promised him, many seasons ago.

Amara foretold of the prophecy after the birth of Rhiannon and Flora, that they would have another set of twins. These twins would be twins of birth only. Their final children would be a boy and a girl. She told them of great things to come and of much sorrow to follow.

†

Amara saw a boy, Bronwen, as dark and yet as pure as Raven had come to be. Bronwen was to follow in her footsteps when he grew older and depart for the seas. She also saw a girl. It had come to be that it was Perta who troubled her mind more than any other had in her life. Perta would inherit all the evil the world had to offer. She would be born without a soul carrying upon her body the birthmark in the shape of a black hawk. Amara saw no good in the girl and no possible redemption.

Upon seeing the soulless unborn child's destiny, she set into motion what she knew she must. Amara informed

227

Pelor of what must be done in the end. He agreed to his part in the plan, even knowing the heartache it would cause all around him.

Amara never told her mother of the evil, soulless child that was to be born, for she did not want to cause her any more sorrow than she had already known in her life. For following her destiny, Amara knew it would in turn destroy her own soul. Knowing her destiny was at hand to be the cause of such untold grief, she forged ahead willingly. For she could not let this evil upon the world and she alone would pay the price for cheating the God of War out of what he was due.

†

Lord Raven stood in the doorway to her twin daughters' room, nothing but love and devotion in her heart. Even if she heard the tale a thousand more times, it would still bring tears to her eyes and joy to her heart. She did not need hear the end of the story she knew how it turned out. It was as it always was…everyone lived happily ever after.

Raven moved to the bed knowing Kat would need help getting up. She gently helped her wife to stand. Rubbing Kat's swollen belly, Raven knew it was time even before Kat did herself. So in tune were their bodies, that she had also felt the first flutter of contraction.

Kataryna stood with her hands on her very swollen belly and gazed up lovingly at her Lord, her wife…her soul. "It is time, my love."

Raven laughed. "I know. I felt the contraction even though I was in the kitchens. Let me say this, Sairana is now cursing my name from the mess she has to clean up from the floor."

Horrified, Kat questioned her. "I am half afraid to ask…"

They quietly made their way from the room. Not wanting to worry Kat, Raven made light of what had happened. "Let me say this…what I felt was not pleasant and if it is anything like what you are feeling it makes me love you all the more that you would suffer through this pain to bear our children. Let me also say I did not react well to pain like that."

†

Kataryna knew full well, how she reacted to pain. "Oh, poor Sairana…please remind me later to thank her for not hitting you with a ladle at the mess you created." Another painful contraction hit her, causing her to almost double over in pain.

"Raven, my love, I really think we need to hurry to our chambers, these little ones will not wait much longer in here." Kat felt her legs about to give out as she grasped Raven's strong arm. "I fear you are going to have to carry me if we are to make it in time. I do not think Bronwen is going to wait another moment to be born."

Kat's knees gave out just as Raven swept her off her feet and rapidly made her way down the hall to their chambers.

†

Entering their private bedchamber, Raven found Amara and Pelor awaiting their arrival. She thought it strange Pelor there, just as she had found it strange that two guards were in the outer chamber. As another pain tore through Kataryna, Raven spared them not another thought and set about to welcome her last two children into the world.

All had now come full circle. Everything was as it should be. The Queen and her Lord ruled with as much love in their hearts for their children and each other as they ruled for the love of their people.

✝

Amara and Pelor knew this sunset would bring about much happiness and untold sorrow. Therefore, with that, they set about their tasks, for the people they loved and what mattered most in the world...Destiny.

Destiny, though, is a tricky thing at best. At times it has a way of fulfilling itself without being asked. With the death of Perta, the Fates and the War God would bide their time until a future heir would be born to take her place.

It would be an heir born into the world through love and devotion. The child, however, would know only heartache and death; being the cause of much of it herself.

Until the time of the birth of the next child with the black hawk marked upon her skin, all the coming generations would know only love and peace.

When the legacy came to pass, she would bring forth with her Chaos, Destruction, and Death.

About the Author

Alane Hotchkin

If anyone knows where the birthplace of oil is in North America you will know exactly where I am talking about. I was born in Oil City, PA and later lived in Pittsburgh. You say do not know where Oil City is. Well, imagine a tiny town, population "two," directly between Pittsburgh & Erie, PA. I grew up with family always around (mostly male) and all with wicked senses of humor. One cousin one day decided to see if his father's (my uncle) car would float in the retention pond.

Okay, so now you also know where I got my sense of humor. My earliest childhood memory is driving to the store with my favorite uncle to buy his cigarettes & booze in his HUGE Cadillac with the top down, while listening to an eight-track of Dolly Parton's *Coat of Many Colors* and so a little girl's education was started. LOL

Side Note: Finally, in 2005 I had to admit to myself and, unwillingly, to others that, well…I'm a country hick even though all my life I tried to be a city girl. LOL

Went to college and majored in Accounting/Business Law/Economic Engineering and guess what, I ended up in the accounting field. Now tell me, how many people actually end up working in the field they studied for? The accounting led to working at a bookstore for five years, a local television station for ten years and then onto where I am now. What can I say, I love numbers.

Contact Alane at Lillithblackhawk121@yahoo.com and visit her website at http://www.alanelhotchkin.com.

Other Books from Affinity eBook Press

Asset Management—Annette Mori Toni, Sophie, and Kim, are the modern day version of Robin Hood blended with the Three Musketeers. For the past eighteen months, they have been moving the assets of the rapacious bank executives to the more deserving coffers—at least in their minds—of the poor and middle class. When a mysterious woman keeps crossing paths with Toni, sparks fly. Is it a coincidence or all part of some greater master plan? Is she friend or foe? Add the Russian mob, the FBI, and an all-female covert organization and you have the perfect recipe for danger, intrigue, and even love. Does the trio join forces with *the organization*? Follow the twists and turns to the explosive conclusion. Not everything is black and white. There are many shades of gray and sometimes it's difficult to decipher who is good and who is evil. No one is all virtue or all malevolence, but sometimes love helps us rise above.

Do Dreams Come True?—JM Dragon Laurel Rogers was unceremoniously dumped by her long-time lover, painter Ronnie Lancaster, finding her belongings outside the apartment they shared. To add to her misery, the next day she loses her job, fired by the Dragon of Finance, Christen

Jamison. What else can go wrong? Oh yes, her best friend becomes engaged to the brother of the Dragon. For ten years, Christen Jamison has never forgiven her partner for walking out on her. She's given up on love, making her work her life as the accountant for the family business. After she is directed to fire a woman who should never have been on the redundancy list—Laurel Rogers—Christen begins to doubt her commitment to the store's management and policies. How do two people who really shouldn't get on end up in a relationship? Find out in this deliciously ordinary romance.

Return to Me—Erin O'Reilly Renowned microbiologist Sydney Tanner left work as normal for her trip home but never arrived. Ellie Scott her wife of ten years franticly to the point of obsession attempts to find her—the only evidence there is something amiss is Syd's crashed truck then the clues go cold. Ellie refuses to believe that she will never see Syd again but realizes many months later with nothing solid to go on, it's time to attempt to move forward with a life without Syd. Leaving home town she accepts a new job at Salvation aptly named for Ellie's predicament. There Ellie meets beautiful Maya Rojas who is the director of Salvation a rehabilitation hospital. Although she hasn't given up on finding Syd, Ellie finds herself increasingly drawn to Maya. However, Salavation isn't all that it appears! Will Ellie find peace and happiness again or does Salvation hold the essential clue to Syd's disappearance? A wonderful romance cloaked within an intriguing mystery.

Terminal Event—Ali Spooner Tally Rainwater was born with the gift of second sight, something she never understood. A near-fatal accident, at age twelve, makes her visions clearer, but not the reason for them. As she matures, Lisa, a spirit, enters her visions to guide her in using her gift, but still not the reason why. After Tally's gift helps locate the body of a murdered teen, she realizes her gift is to help lost souls find their peace. When it's discovered, a serial killer murdered the teen, Blair "Spooky" Cooper is the Agent in Charge assigned to the case. A task force of local detectives and FBI forms to track the killer. Blair enlists the aid of Tally, and together with the team, Tally helps them piece together the puzzle of murders spanning twenty years throughout the Deep South. Even with the complication of the case, Blair and Tally have an undeniable attraction to each other. As they close in on the killer, the killer focuses on Tally, jeopardizing her bond with Blair and everyone around her. For the sake of the case, they put their attraction on the back burner until the killer is caught. Will the killer be caught or continue to evade authorities? Can Tally and Blair's budding romance survive the possibility? Read this intense murder mystery romance and find out.

Arc Over Time—Jen Silver_ Dr Kathryn Moss has job offers flowing in after her exciting archaeological discoveries at Starling Hill the previous year. Now she has choices to make that could jeopardise her relationship with Denise Sullivan, the fiery journalist, who has become her lover. For Denise the choice seems obvious. She thinks they have moved beyond the casual sex stage to something more like a true relationship. However, she's not sure how to handle Kathryn's continuing infatuation with Ellie Winters. Ellie's new career as a promising artist proves to be a catalyst for the simmering tensions in relations between her wife Robin, Kathryn, and Denise. Will Denise persevere in her pursuit of the reluctant professor? Does Ellie have anything to fear from Kathryn's fascination with her art, or is there another motive behind the professor's obsessive interest? This wonderful romantic continuation with the characters from *Starting Over* ties up loose ends. But the question is—does everyone have a happy ending? A must read.

Presence—Charlene Neal After catching her husband red-handed in bed with his secretary, Kayleigh Gibbs takes her daughter and her Jeep and flees across the country. She opens up her own veterinarian practice, and they move into an old, secluded farmhouse in Hoekwil, South Africa. At her best friend's housewarming party Kayleigh meets the beautiful and enchanting Rebecca Steward. Rebecca is instantly drawn to Kayleigh, but is still recovering from a breakup—her girlfriend left her for a man. She's afraid of a repeat performance with Kayleigh, and won't pursue a romantic relationship with her, preferring instead to develop a platonic friendship. When odd, inexplicable things start happening on the farmhouse, a terrified Kayleigh turns to Rebecca for comfort, only to find herself developing unexplainable feelings for her new friend. Rebecca, despite her best intentions, is falling in love with Kayleigh. But when Rebecca moves in with Kayleigh to help her get to the bottom of the haunting, she finds more than she bargained for. Can Rebecca and Kayleigh overcome ghosts from the past and their own insecurities, or will a presence from the past tear them apart?

A Walk Away—Lacey Schmidt Kat and Rand's daily worlds are 2,100 miles apart, but something about their meeting on the magical shores of the nation's oldest national park east of the Mississippi sparks questions that neither woman can just walk away without answering. Sometimes chance brings you to the right person to help you resolve some of your baggage, and you learn to like yourself a little more. Kat and Rand are smart enough to recognize this chance in each other, but they also find that there is a catch to every opportunity—walking toward something is always walking away from something else.

Love Forever, Live Forever—Annette Mori No one forgets their first love. For Nicky, that's Sara, who abruptly disappears one day, leaving only a cryptic letter. That day scarred her soul. When the pain starts to diminish, Nicky begins to get her life back on track until it is derailed once again by an unimaginable twist. Changed forever, Nicky becomes a careless, womanizing nomad known as the Little Wild One, until she meets Annie. Thirteen years later, Nicky's finally settled and happy. Fate intervenes and puts her directly back into the path of her first love, Sara, and the corresponding events send her into a tailspin. Now she must decide—who will be the person she ends up living with and loving forever?

Possessing Morgan—Erica Lawson New York City, in the height of summer. Crime seems to have taken a holiday, and Detective Morgan O'Callaghan is bored, bored, bored. Paperwork is mating and multiplying on her desk, and even a jaywalker is starting to look good. Anything to get her out from behind her desk! Enter Andrea Worthington, Charleston socialite and all-around rich girl, right down to the wealthy fiancé. She's also the new Assistant District Attorney assigned to Morgan's precinct. Their first meeting is like two freight trains crashing head on. Then a high profile, career make-or-break murder case throws them together again. The investigation has barely begun when Andrea becomes the target of a nearly fatal hit-and-run. But was it really aimed at her? Can she and Morgan find the common ground they need to solve the case and stop the attacks, or are the gaps just too wide to bridge?

Twenty-three Miles—Renee MacKenzie Talia Lisher has a long family history of lying, about anything and everything. With her father dead, and her mom gone on a quest to start a new life, Talia struggles to keep in touch with her only remaining family, her incarcerated brother. When Talia sets her sights on Officer Shay Eliot, she vows to stop lying. She starts watching Shay, waiting for just the right circumstances and amount of courage to talk to her. Talia might be watching Shay, but someone in a dark van is watching Talia. Is the mystery driver a dangerous part of her family's past, or is it all just a coincidence? Shay Eliot has left the police force because of what she perceives as a hostile work environment. When a brutal double-murder on the 23-mile-long Colonial Parkway puts the FBI's magnifying glass squarely on her, her alibi comes from an unlikely source – a young woman who has been stalking her. Shay wants to keep her distance from Talia, but once she gets to know the younger woman she can't keep feelings from developing. This is a story about community, and how it comes together in dangerous and devastating times. When you don't know who to trust, you better have friends who will rally around you. Will Talia and Shay find the answers they need to the mystery of the murders on the parkway, or will justice be elusive? Will they survive their quest for the truth?

Confined Spaces—Renee MacKenzie Andie Waters spends her days pulling waste samples for environmental testing and at night, she tends bar at The Cave, a popular hangout for straights in a small Georgia town. Serial monogamy has grown stale for her, so she's content working to pay off her debts and hanging out with her old hound dog. Or so she thinks, until a beautiful lesbian drops by The Cave. Andie suspects her involvement with the woman will be only temporary. Little does she know no part of her life will be left untouched. Kara Travis likewise anticipates nothing more than a brief fling upon meeting Andie, especially given her reputation as both a personal ice princess and a corporate hatchet wielder for Royal Environmental. What luck to find a hot lesbian bartender in nowhere rural Georgia. Andie and Kara spend a passionate weekend together and find that their notions of no strings attached are far from accurate. Their supposed short-term ideal diversion of a commitment-free romp hits a major complication when they come face-to-face with one another at Royal Environmental's offices Monday morning. While carrying out her duties, Kara discovers crimes being committed by and against Royal Environmental employees. Will Kara be forced to shut down the Georgia Division of the company? If she does, Andie will lose her job. Worse yet, Kara may lose Andie before she's really even sure she's got her. Corporate politics, complicated romance, and long distances conspire to keep Andie and Kara all boxed in. Can love triumph despite the Confined Spaces?

Reece's Star—TJ Vertigo Reece Corbett watches over the dancers in her gentleman's club with the blue, razor sharp eyes of The Animal. Few know that resting comfortably in her office is her newest love, a tiny MinPin named Smudge. What happened to The Animal, known for her rapacious appetite for women and danger? Faith Ashford is what happened to The Animal. Faith and Reece have been together a while now and they have settled into something resembling domestic bliss. This bliss alarms Reece. It's one thing for Faith to see her softer side, that's vulnerability enough, but to let her friends see it…no. Not the best plan. Under Faith's guiding, loving hand, will Reece successfully traverse the rocky road of emotion and embrace the positive changes in her life? Or will she panic and be unable to control that Animal part of herself? Will she take that next step to declare herself fully capable of love and devotion? This third installment in the popular series that began with *Private Dancer* continues the passionate and often hilarious romance of Reece and Faith as they both grow in love and in trust.

Flight—Renee Mackenzie It's 1983 and Kate Hunter is a student at a small, private college in Virginia. When Lana coaxes her onto the back of her beat-up scooter one night, Kate's education starts to encompass more than just her pre-vet studies. Kate has always done as expected of her, so when she starts staying away from home on weekends to spend time with her new lover it's way out of character for her. Lana is secretive, but Kate accepts things as they are and gives Lana her space. When she feels the sting of betrayal, will she be able to continue giving Lana her privacy? Kate's sister April is a high school student playing with fire as she parties with her older boyfriend, Boyd. After finding someone overdosed the morning after a big party, April grows weary of all the drugs and alcohol. Will she be able to convince Boyd that they should slow down? Will she be able to pull it together before it's too late? Kate and April are forced to face up to events from their younger years, their mother's desertion, and their long-deteriorating relationship with one another. Some lives will be lost and others changed forever when the sisters' lives intersect. Will they be consumed by the wreckage, or will they be able to pick themselves up and take flight?

Reflected Passion—Erica Lawson **Where passion, reality, and destiny combine**. Dale Wincott is a 27-year-old woman born into Bostonian wealth and groomed to marry into the social hierarchy. Her mother is a hard-hearted society matriarch, but her father feels for his daughter and helps Dale find a life on her own as a furniture restorer. Françoise Marie Aurélie de Villerey is a 28-year-old Countess, born into the French aristocracy and forced to marry a count much older than herself. For ten years, she was his trophy wife, forced to endure his perverted desires, until the day he finally died. He had broken her emotionally and she no longer cared for what life had to offer, slipping from one sexual partner to another as often as she changed her clothes. Until... that one night when Françoise looked up during a sexual encounter and saw Dale watching her from the mirror. A veritable angel, full of innocence and curiosity, who touched her very soul. Through the mirror, Françoise embraces life anew, while for Dale it is a powerful awakening, forcing her to discover not only her sensual nature, but the inner strength she possesses.

E-Books, Print, Free e-books

Visit our website for more publications available online.

www.affinityebooks.com

Published by Affinity E-Book Press NZ LTD
Canterbury, New Zealand

Registered Company 2517228

www.ingramcontent.com/pod-product-compliance
Lightning Source LLC
Chambersburg PA
CBHW060545260626
47161CB00003B/1056

* 9 7 8 0 9 0 8 3 5 1 2 8 2 *